MORE FAVOURITE
ANIMAL TALES

Also by Jill Tomlinson

MORE FAVOURITE ANIMAL TALES

The Gorilla Who
Wanted to
Grow Up

The Penguin
Who Wanted
to Find Out

The Aardvark
Who Wasn't Sure

JILL TOMLINSON

Pictures by Paul Howard

EGMONT

EGMONT

We bring stories to life

The Gorilla Who Wanted To Grow Up:
To Rolfe, my beloved gorilla, and the rest of the troop; and, of course, D.H.
The Penguin Who Wanted To Find Out:
*For David, who has been to the Antarctic, his wife, Pat, and the boys,
James, Peter and Mathew, and of course Claudius.*
The Aardvark Who Wasn't Sure:
*For D.L. and his children Claire, Annushka and Tamara,
not forgetting the D that I never leave out, D.H.*

This edition published 2008
by Egmont UK Limited
239 Kensington High Street
London W8 6SA

The Gorilla Who Wanted To Grow Up first published in Great Britain 1977 by Methuen
Children's Books Ltd. Text copyright © 1977 The Estate of Jill Tomlinson.
The Penguin Who Wanted To Find Out first published in Great Britain in 1975 by
Methuen Children's Books Ltd. Text copyright © 1975 The Estate of Jill Tomlinson.
The Aardvark Who Wasn't Sure first published in Great Britain in 1973 by Methuen
Children's Books Ltd. Text copyright © 1973 The Estate of Jill Tomlinson.
Illustration copyright © Paul Howard 2004

ISBN 978 1 4052 3731 4

3 5 7 9 10 8 6 4

www.egmont.co.uk

A CIP catalogue record for this title is available from the British Library

Typeset by Avon DataSet Ltd, Bidford on Avon, Warwickshire
Printed and bound in Great Britain by the CPI Group

The Gorilla Who Wanted to Grow Up

JILL TOMLINSON

Pictures by Paul Howard

EGMONT

Contents

Pongo

Pongo was a young gorilla. He lived in the mountains of Africa. He had long glossy black hair and a black shiny nose. His arms were long and he walked on the knuckles of his hands on all fours. He could stand upright like a man but he didn't walk very far or very often like this.

Pongo lived in a troop of gorillas and his father was the leader. Pongo called him Da but the other gorillas called him the Big Boss. Da looked quite different from Pongo, apart from being much bigger. There were white hairs all over his back mixed with the black ones, so his back looked silver. Pongo's troop passed other

troops sometimes and the leader always had a silver back like Da. Pongo often wondered why.

When Pongo was younger he lived with his mother but now that he was growing up he spent much more time with Da. Sometimes he leaned against him for his afternoon nap.

One day Pongo felt Da stirring and knew that he could ask him some questions. 'Da,' he said, 'will I have a silver back like you?'

'Yes, when you're a big chap like me,' said Da.

'When will that be?' Pongo asked.

'Oh, when you're ten or eleven, I think.'

'How old am I now?' Pongo asked.

'I don't really know,' Da said. 'I've forgotten. But you're tall already so I don't think it can be very long before you have a silver back.'

'Will I get a big chest like you?' Pongo asked. 'And be able to thump it? I've always wanted to do that.'

'Yes, you will,' da said, 'but not just yet. You'll have to wait a little while. When you're grown up you'll be in charge of the troop yourself.'

'A troop of my own?' Pongo said. 'with my own wives and children?'

'That's it,' Da said. 'Now I want to sleep some more. Go and play with your friends.'

Pongo went off to play with the other young gorillas. They always had a good game when the grown-ups were sleeping. There were lots of things to do in the rain forest where they lived. They could climb up and down the trees and swing on the creepers that hung from the trees. They could chase each other and fight – but very gently because gorillas never hurt each other. When one of them had had enough he crouched down and held one of his arms across the back of his neck. This always stopped the fight.

Pongo was sitting under a tree wondering what to do when something hurled itself at him.

'You lazy·lump,' it cried. The something was Zambi, Pongo's best friend.

'I'm not lazy,' Pongo said. 'I was just deciding what to do.'

'Well you're a jolly slow decider,' Zambi said. 'I've decided I'm going to roll you over that cliff.'

'What cliff?' Pongo asked. 'That miserable little bank over there?'

They began wrestling on the top of the bank. They enjoyed fighting because they

were almost exactly the same size. Zambi
suddenly rolled over and Pongo was jerked
over the bank. It was in fact a slippery slope.
It was great fun sliding down.

'Zambi!' Pongo called. 'Come and join
me. This is great fun.'

Zambi was already just behind him.
'There, you see what a good friend
I am,' he said. 'This is a lovely
place for a game.'

It was, too. It was difficult getting back up again but they soon found some bushes and creepers to pull themselves up with. They went on playing there until they were tired. Sitting at the bottom Zambi said, 'We must tell the others about this.'

'Not yet,' Pongo said. 'I've been talking to Da and I want to tell you what he told me.' And that's what he did.

'So you want a silver back?' Zambi said. 'Don't you want to play games any more? The Boss doesn't play games very much.'

'Well, he can't,' Pongo said. 'His job is too look after us all. I suppose when I have a silver back I'll be too busy to play games. No, you're right. I'll just enjoy being what I am for the moment.'

He did, too. He got Zambi to climb on to

a rock and then tried to push him off it. This was a favourite game of theirs. I'm the King of the Castle. Then they noticed the Big Boss getting up and reaching round him for food. It was eating time. They stopped playing and began to do the same themselves. This was a good part of the forest because there was food everywhere. Gorillas eat nettles and leaves of all kinds and the pulp out of the stems of plants; even bark off trees. And in this part of the forest they hardly had to move to find more food. They were surrounded by it and they ate and ate until they could eat no more.

After he'd finished eating, the Big Boss began to make himself a nest. That only meant picking up a few bundles of leaves and putting them round him. He laid down to go to sleep then. All the other gorillas copied him.

It was sleeping time. That was what his job was, to show everybody what to do and when to do it. The Big Boss himself always slept on the ground now because he was too big and heavy. But Pongo was still light enough to sleep up a tree. He made a nest with his mother. She had a surprise for him tonight.

'You won't be able to sleep with me much longer, Pongo,' she said. 'You're going to have to sleep on the ground like Da.'

'I know I'm getting bigger,' Pongo said, 'but can't we make a stronger nest?'

'Not strong enough for three,' Ma said.

'Three?' Pongo said. 'You mean we're going to have another baby?'

'That's right,' Ma said.

'When?' Pongo asked.

'Oh, I don't know that, but quite soon,'

Ma said. 'And you can help me look after it.'

'You've got Da,' Pongo said.

'But Da's very busy. I think I shall need you sometimes,' Ma said. 'But come on, let's go to sleep now. goodnight, Pongo.'

'Goodnight, Ma,' Pongo said.

So they went to sleep in their nest and Da went to sleep at the bottom of the tree.

Man

The next morning the sun was shining. The Big Boss was feeling lazy and had breakfast in bed. That wasn't difficult. All he had to do was reach out and pick some celery. Pongo was just getting ready to climb down the tree and join him when Da roared, and that was quite a noise. He stood up on his hind legs and stuck out his great chest and threw bits of celery in the air. Then he began to thump ths palms of his hands on his chest. It made a sound like a war-drum echoing through the forest, making all the gorillas sit up and listen.

'Don't move,' Pongo's mother said. 'That means danger.'

'Danger?' Pongo said. 'What danger? You told me we've only got one enemy. Man.'

'Yes,' his mother said. 'What do you think that is over there?'

Then Pongo saw the man. He was standing under a tree looking at them.

'It's all right, Ma,' said Pongo. 'He hasn't got a gun or a spear.'

'No, he hasn't, has he?' Ma said. 'But let's wait and see what Da decides.'

Da charged at the man, throwing up leaves as he went. The man didn't move. He seemed to be enjoying the war dance.

Da stopped and stared at the man for a moment and then went back to his nest and went on eating.

Ma laughed. 'That man's seen gorillas before,' she said. 'Men usually run away when they see Da charging like that. But he just stood still. Da's eating now, so he doesn't think the man is dangerous. Come on, we'll go and have our breakfast too.'

So Pongo and his mother climbed down the tree and began eating. They stayed near Da though. The rest of the gorillas stayed near the Big Boss too. Although he was waiting, the Big Boss kept an eye on the man.

Zambi came over to Pongo. 'Why is that man watching us like that?' he said. 'Perhaps he thinks we're dangerous, and that's why he's keeping a little way away.'

'No,' Pongo said. 'He's not afraid of us because he didn't move when Da charged him.'

They went on eating like Da. But when they were full Zambi said to Pongo: 'He's still watching us, that man. Let's go and watch him.'

They crept a bit closer to him, keeping well hidden behind a thicket.

'Look,' whispered Zambi. 'He's pulling something out of that bag. Perhaps it's a gun.'

'I don't think you eat guns,' Pongo said. 'and that's what he's doing. Anyway, I don't think guns are little white things like that.'

It was just a sandwich.

'I'd like to try one of those things,' said Zambi.

'Gorillas don't pinch each others food,' Pongo said. 'So we don't pinch man's food either.'

14

Just then the man reached into his bag and pulled something else out.

'Look, it's a banana,' Pongo said. 'He's peeling it and eating it.'

'Ugh! Doesn't he know that the only |nice part of the banana tree is the pulp out of the stem.'

They went back and told Da about this funny man.

'I don't think he's very dangerous,' Pongo said. 'But it's fun watching him.'

'Well, you do that,' said Da. 'Watch him. You have to learn about man. Know your enemy is a good rule.'

'He's not an enemy,' Pongo said.

'No, I don't think he is,' Da said. 'And that makes it easier to watch him safely. So you go and learn about him.'

'I've just learned something,' said Zambi. 'From here. Look. He's taller than Da.'

They all looked at him.

'He's as thin as a creeper, though,' said Pongo. 'Da must be ten times as wide as he is.'

'Well, he's not a creeper, so don't try to climb him,' said Da. 'I don't think he could take your weight. He's quite old; look at his hair.'

They looked.

'It's white,' Pongo said. 'And he has lines on his face just like a very old gorilla.'

'Yes, he's old,' Da said. 'Only old men have white hair. So you be gentle with him.'

'I don't know,' Zambi said to Pongo. 'Your Da's getting old too. Now we've got to be gentle with our enemies.'

'He's not an enemy,' Pongo said. 'Da knows what he's doing. You get wiser as you get older, usually.'

'Oh, of course, you'd know that,' Zambi said. 'Well, a wise old man like you . . .'

'Someone round here,' interrupted Pongo, 'seems to be asking for a fight.' And that's what they had, till they decided to go on eating as usual.

Later Da began to make his nest. Pongo began to make one near Zambi.

'I thought you slept up the tree with your mother?' Zambi said.

'No, I'm getting too heavy,' Pongo said. 'May I stay near you?'

'Yes,' Zambi said. 'It will be nice to have company.'

'Is the man making a nest?' Pongo said.

'I don't expect so,' said Zambi. 'Men don't like to make nests near fierce gorillas

like me!' And, sure enough, when they sat in
their nests afterwards the man had gone.

Whoopsie

The next morning after breakfast Pongo set
out to see if he could find the man. Da had
told him to look for a big nest made of tree
trunks. Pongo found it and he was amazed.
This wasn't like one of their nests because
it had a sort of top to it. That man wasn't
going to get wet when it rained! There didn't
seem to be anyone near the nest so Pongo
looked through a hole in the side of it. He

was so surprised at what he saw that he rushed straight back to Da to tell him about it.

'That man,' he said. 'He was taking the fur off his face with a sort of scratcher thing. I think he must have done his chest and arms as well, because he was quite bare.'

Da laughed. 'Men are bare,' he said. 'That's why they put coverings on to keep warm. they haven't got nice warm coats like us. Oh look, here he comes now. Shall I do a war dance, do you think?'

'No,' Pongo said. 'You know he's safe to have around.'

'Well, keep an eye on him for me, Pongo,' Da said. 'I want to get on with my breakfast. But I don't think he's going to be any trouble.'

Pongo didn't watch the man very much. He was hungry and wanted to get on with his breakfast. Gorillas need to eat an awful lot, because they only eat plants and things and they need a lot to make them strong. Pongo was so busy eating he forgot all about the man.

Then something began to puzzle him. Usually Da took them a little way away from where they had eaten a day before, but he hadn't today. There was plenty of food so they didn't really need to move, but it was puzzling.

They found out the reason at rest-time. It was a very nice reason. Ma had been having her baby. Pongo saw his mother coming towards Da with something in her arms. Something with bare arms which were hanging round her neck.

'Look!' Pongo said to Zambi. 'Look!'

Ma handed the little bare baby to Da

and he stroked it and then handed it back.

'She's lovely,' he said. 'Now you go and sit in the shade.'

'I've got a sister,' Pongo said. 'A baby sister. I wonder what we're going to call her. I'll go and ask Da.'

'We haven't decided yet,' said Da. 'I expect we will later on.'

Pongo and Zambi were watching Ma with the baby and Zambi said to Pongo, 'I thought babies rode on their mother's backs.'

'Not very new babies,' Pongo said. 'They're not strong enough to hang on. Ma will carry her until she's strong enough.'

'You seem to know an awful lot,' Zambi said. 'Where did you find that out?'

'We see other troops going past,' Pongo said.

'I don't take much notice of other troops,' Zambi said.

'No, you're too busy eating,' said Pongo. 'That makes me wonder. How is Ma going to eat with her arms full of baby? Perhaps I'd better feed her.'

He went and asked Da.

'No, that's all right, son,' he said. 'She'll hold the baby with one arm and eat with the other one. She's not as greedy as you; she doesn't need to stuff her food in with both hands. She'll manage.'

So they went on eating and later on had a rest in the sun. Gorillas love the sun so when there is any they enjoy it. But Zambi had a surprise; the man was sunbathing too.

'Look,' he said to Pongo. 'Our man. He's got a spotted rump. He's taken off his arm coverings and his leg coverings and he's lying in the sun like us.'

Pongo looked lazily over at the man. 'Yes, you're right. He has a spotted rump like a leopard and he likes the sun like us. That's something we've learned about man.'

Of course, man was wearing his swimming trunks but the gorillas didn't know that.

Nothing much happened for the rest of that day and it was too hot to move. At bedtime Pongo made a nest for his mother. He chose a tree with a fork very low down. Pongo began to bend the branches in all round the fork and this made a very good nest. He was growing up and knew what he was doing. But not quite. He came down the tree to Da.

'Da,' he said, 'how will Ma get the baby

into the nest? She can't climb up a tree holding a baby.'

'You go and fetch her and I'll show you,' Da said.

So Pongo fetched his mother and sister. He understood as soon as he got back to the tree. Da was tall and he could reach the nest easily.

'Can I hold my sister while you climb up to the nest I've made you?' Pongo said.

'Yes, of course you can,' Ma said. 'Here you are.'

'Isn't she tiny?' Pongo said to Da, holding his little sister against his chest.

'She's really small.'

'She'll grow up very quickly,' said Da. 'You'll see.'

Ma called down from the nest. 'Ready.'

Pongo stood under the tree. 'Da,' he said, 'I'm tall enough to hand her up myself.'

'I had a feeling you might be,' he said. 'All right, you give her to Ma.'

Pongo gave his little sister one last hug and then he said, 'Now, up you go. One, two, three, whoopsie,' and handed her up to Ma.

'Whoopsie,' Da said. 'That's a nice name. shall we call her Whoopsie, Ma?'

'Yes,' she said, and holding Whoopsie to her she said, 'There, your brother's named you. Pongo says you're to be called Whoopsie.'

While they were making their own nests Pongo said to Da, 'Whoopsie is tiny and she's so bare, she's as bare as that man.'

Da laughed. 'She won't be for long,' he said. 'She'll have a coat like yours in a week or two. You'll see.'

The Job

Da was quite right about Whoopsie. She was soon covered with black hair and not bare any more. She was soon riding on her mother's back, too. Then one day Pongo saw Ma with no baby on her back. Where was Whoopsie? Pongo rushed over and then he saw that Whoopsie was happily lying on the ground while her mother was eating.

'Is she safe down there?' Pongo asked Ma.

'Of course she is,' Ma said. 'She'll be crawling before long. But she can't learn to do that on my back. She's got to be on the ground.'

Pongo understood, but he ate near them for a bit because he wanted to be quite sure that Whoopsie was safe. He was just pulling up a fern to take a bite when he felt a hand on his shoulder. He looked round to find Da.

'You're a good lad, Pongo,' he said. 'But you know it's just possible that Ma knows what she's doing. Whoopsie isn't her first baby.'

'I just wanted to be sure they were safe,' Pongo said. 'And I didn't know you were near.'

'I wasn't,' Da said. 'But I think this is a good moment for me to ask you something that I've been meaning to ask you for a little while now.'

'Yes?' Pongo said, putting down his fern.

'Well, it's like this,' Da said. 'You're getting to be a big chap now; you've begun to shoot.'

'Shoot?' Pongo said. 'What does that mean? I haven't got a gun.'

'No, you're growing very much taller, which means that you're growing up. Now this is what I want to ask you. You and Zambi are the two oldest of the youngsters and I need you to help me. Lately we've been staying round the same bit of forest because it's very good here, but sometimes we make a sort of procession to move along a path to a new place. Now I need someone I can trust at the very back, a sentinel.'

'A what?' asked Pongo.

'A rear guard. Someone who can make sure that it's safe at the back of the procession. Zambi can help and you can work together. It's very important. I'll go at the front leading the procession; then there's Ma and Whoopsie and all the females and the youngsters. I must be sure that the back is safe. You must warn me if anything dangerous comes near. That means you must roar and bang your chest. Or perhaps you had better bang the stump of a tree, because you haven't got a very big chest yet. Anyway, we shan't be moving for a day or two so you and Zambi can practise. Will you do this for me?'

'Oh, yes,' Pongo said. 'My chest seems bigger already. I feel much more grown up having a real job to do.'

'Well, go and tell Zambi about it,' Da said. 'I'll look after Ma and Whoopsie for you.'

Pongo rushed off to find Zambi, banging his chest hard all the way. Zambi ran to meet him.

'What's the matter?' he said. 'Danger?'

Pongo laughed. 'No, I'm just practising,' he said. 'We've got a job, you and I.' And he told Zambi all about it.

For the next few days all the other gorillas spent a lot of time huddling round the Big Boss because Pongo and Zambi were roaring and thumping trees and their chests. Da explained to the rest of the gorillas that Pongo and Zambi were only practising, but some of them were still a bit frightened very time they started. And that was often, because Pongo and Zambi were practising whenever they weren't eating or sleeping. Pongo soon had a great big roar, but Zambi hadn't.

'Well, I'm younger than you,' he said to Pongo.

'Yes,' Pongo said. 'And you're good at tree-banging. With two of us at it we can

warn Da. That's what matters.'

One day Da came up and inspected them.

'Well, I think you can stop practising now,' he said. 'Some of the old girls are in a perpetual state of fright.'

'There's nothing for them to be afraid of, anyway,' Pongo said. 'We haven't seen a thing.'

'No, it's pretty safe up here in the mountains,' Da said, 'though sometimes you get men with spears and things like that. Very, very occasionally you find a leopard, but usually they keep well away from us. A chap like me can tear a leopard in half and they know it.'

'What about the creeper,' Zambi said. 'Do we have to roar for him?' the creeper was the name they used for the man because he was so thin.

Da laughed. 'No,' he said. 'He seems to be one of the troop now; he's always with us. I think he'd better be in front of you so you can keep him safe. A leopard might go for him. Well now you can go and play. You're off duty. But I'll tell you when I need you.'

So that's how it was. A few days later Da took them along a path to a new place and he asked Pongo and Zambi to bring up the rear of the troop. The man didn't seem a bit surprised to find Pongo and Zambi behind him when he had tacked on to the back of the troop.

There was only one awkward moment that morning. Another troop passed them going the other way. The other leader and Da exchanged nods and that was all right. But when the other leader saw the man he stopped. He was just beginning to pull up some leaves to throw into the air before he roared when, to Pongo's amazement, the man nodded his head from side to side. That is the gorilla sign for 'we mean no harm'. So Pongo nodded as well, and Zambi did too. Then, the leader of the other troop went on past them.

'Where did you learn to do that?' Zambi asked Pongo.

'Watching other troops,' Pongo said. 'and that's where the man learned it too, I suppose. I told you he must have been with gorillas before. He's a clever old chap.'

When they reached the place where Da had been leading them soon afterwards, they found it was a field full of blackberries. They sat around stuffing their mouths with fruit

until they could eat no more. Then they all
fell asleep.

They made their nests that night in the
forest near to the field. There wasn't a black-
berry left by the time they had finished.

Fun and games

Life went on as usual in their new surroundings.
But one day Pongo had a surprise. He was
having a little snooze with all the others when
he felt something tugging at him. He looked
down sleepily and then his eyes nearly
popped out. It was Whoopsie. Where had she
come from? Ma was some way away.

'What are you doing here?' Pongo asked.

'Pongo,' she said, and tugged at him

again. She wanted him to play with her.
Whoopsie had been growing up and she could
crawl now. That's how she had reached Pongo.
Ma was a very long way away. Well, Pongo
played with her. It was quite clear that that's
what Whoopsie thought brothers were for. He
rolled her over and over. She liked that. And
he threw her up and down and caught her.

'Now, come on, climb on my back and
I'll give you a ride back to Ma. She'll be
wondering where you are,' Pongo said after
a while.

Whoopsie didn't understand straight away
but he lay on his tummy and of course she
climbed onto him. Then he said 'Now hang
on tight, I'm going to give you a bumpy ride.'
And he crawled over to Ma. Whoopsie loved it.

When Ma saw them coming she laughed.

'Whoopsie's been growing up and you hadn't even noticed, had you, Pongo?' she said.

'No, I hadn't,' Pongo said. 'But how did she find me? I thought baby gorillas couldn't see very well.'

'Oh, Whoopsie can now,' Ma said. 'She watches you every day playing with your friends. She's dying to join you. In fact I was going to ask you, do you think she could play with you today?'

'She's too little,' Pongo said. 'She'll get knocked over and trodden on.'

'Not with her big brother to look after her,' Ma said.

'Oh, all right,' Pongo said. 'She can come on my back for the difficult bits.'

At playtime when Ma and Da lay down for a nap Pongo put Zambi at the front of a follow-my-leader and he came at the back carrying Whoopsie. At first they swung on creepers and Pongo found that Whoopsie could do that by herself. She had strong little arms and she could hang on. Then they did some running and jumping and for that Pongo carried Whoopsie on his back. When Zambi climbed a tree, Pongo began climbing it too with Whoopsie on his back. But Whoopsie had a surprise for him. She was much lighter than he was. She jumped off his back and ran up the tree ahead of him, much higher than he could go. But it was the first time she had ever climbed a tree and she got stuck.

'Go on without us,' Pongo called to the others. 'Whoopsie's stuck so I've got to rescue her.'

He had quite a job, too. The branches

were much too thin to take his weight so he couldn't climb up and fetch her. He had to get her down some other way.

'Now, Whoopsie, this game is called follow-my-leader and you have to follow me and I'm going down. Now come on,' Pongo called up to her.

Pongo put his arms round the trunk and slid down to the bottom. Whoopsie did not move. Ma was there watching and laughing.

'It's all right, Pongo,' she said. 'I'll fetch Whoopsie. I'm much lighter than you and I can get up there.'

But Da said, 'No, Ma, you stay here
and we'll see if Pongo can get her down.
He's no fool.'

'But she'll get frightened,' Ma said. 'I
must go to her.'

'No,' Pongo said. 'Da is right. I know
what he means. Whoopsie wants to feel that
she's like the rest of us now and not a baby
any more. If Ma fetches her she's still a baby
and she won't like that.'

Da looked at Ma. 'Pongo's growing up,
too,' he said. 'He's going to be a good brother
for Whoopsie. Let's see what he'll do next.'

Pongo was already half way up the tree
again. He got as high as he could and then
he called up to Whoopsie.

'Come on, there's a place just behind you
where you can put your foot. Look down and

find it. I can see better than you from here and I'll tell you where to put your feet. You just hang on with your arms and do what I tell you. You're a big girl now, you can do it.'

'I'm frightened,' she said.

'Rubbish,' said Pongo. 'I'll catch you if you fall, but you won't. You're a good climber. Now, come on. Put your foot where I said.'

Whoopsie did that, and in a few minutes she was down as far as Pongo was.

'I did it,' she said. 'I did it.'

'I knew you could,' Pongo said. 'You're not a baby any more, are you? You're a big girl. Now this last bit you can't do because your arms aren't long enough to go right round the tree. So just put them round my neck and I'll take you down on my back.'

So they slid down like that together and

then Pongo ran after the others to catch them up.

'Come on, Ma,' said Da. 'I think we can leave Pongo to look after Whoopsie.'

'I can see that,' Ma said. 'I don't seem to be needed round here any more.'

Da laughed. 'I don't think Pongo is going to be able to give Whoopsie her milk,' he said. 'Now now or ever. So Whoopsie will need you as much as I do.' And he put his arm round her and led her away.

Ma looked up at Da. 'You're right,' she said. 'But Pongo is a good brother. He'll teach her a lot. And she's so pleased that now she can play with the others. It's a shame that there aren't any babies her own size for her to play with.'

'Pongo understands that,' Da said.

'That's why he's helping. Look, there's a nice sunny spot over there. Let's have a nap.'

So they went to lie down while Pongo chased after the others with Whoopsie on his back.

Lessons

From then on, Whoopsie played with the other young gorillas every day, and poor Pongo became her teacher. He couldn't play with the others any more because he had to keep an eye on his little sister. Sometimes they played at fighting and Whoopsie was much too small. So when the bigger ones started to fight, Pongo found her a creeper to swing on. Whoopsie loved that.

The difficult thing was tree-climbing.
Whoopsie couldn't forget the time she had
got stuck. Pongo thought Whoopsie a good
climber and wanted to get her climbing
again. So one day he put her on his back
and clambered up the first part of a tree.

'Now, Whoopsie,' he said, 'you go up
the next bit on your own. I can't do that,
but you can.'

'Yes,' Whoopsie said.

But what she climbed was his head. She
stood on his shoulders and hung on to his ears.

'I've done it,' she said.

'You haven't done anything,' said Pongo.

'I have,' said Whoopsie, 'You said I was
to climb up the next bit.'

'Of the tree, not me,' Pongo said.

But Whoopsie wasn't moving, so Pongo

slid down to the ground with Whoopsie still on his shoulders.

'I could climb down this tree, too,' Whoopsie said, climbing down his back and clutching handfuls of fur as she went.

Zambi was laughing at the bottom. 'Poor Pongo,' he said. 'So now you're a tree!'

'Very funny,' said Pongo. 'Now look here, Zambi, you must help me.'

So they hatched a plot. Next day, Pongo climbed another tree with Whoopsie on his back. He told her to go a little way up and come back to him.

'You know I can't do that,' she said.

Pongo grinned across at Zambi, who was up the next tree and had been told what to say.

'She can't do that,' Zambi said, 'she's only a baby.'

That was enough for Whoopsie. She
quickly went up to where Pongo had pointed.
Then, more slowly, she came back to him.
Pongo looked at Zambi. 'There, she's no baby,'
he said. 'I told you she was a good climber.'

There was no stopping Whoopsie now.
Up and down she went like a yo-yo. Then she
tried to climb down to the ground.

'This is the wrong sort of tree for you,'
said Pongo. 'It's too wide for you to get your
arms around. We'll find a better tree
tomorrow that you can climb up and down.'

Pongo gave Whoopsie a tree-climbing
lesson every day. Soon she could get higher
than anyone else, because she was so small.

Running was another thing that Pongo
had to teach his little sister. Whoopsie still
crawled on her knees like a human baby.

'Straighten your legs at the back,' Pongo said, 'and curl your hands on the ground, so that you walk on your knuckles like I do. You can run much faster like that.'

Pongo had to work hard that day, because Whoopsie kept falling over when she ran after the others. He walked swiftly behind her at the back of the pack and picked her up when she fell. She soon learned to walk on her four feet.

'She learns very quickly,' said Pongo. 'You never have to tell her anything more than once.'

'Maybe,' said Zambi, 'but I find it very boring because there's nobody left for me to fight with.'

'Yes, there is,' said Pongo. 'Whoopsie's tired now, so I'll take her back to Ma.'

Then they had a good fight. It was true

that Pongo and Zambi could not play with the others in the way that they used to. They were both getting too big.

One day they were all playing follow-my-leader, a favourite game. In the middle of the game they crawled over Ma's tummy. She was used to this, and didn't mind at all. But Zambi was much too heavy, so he jumped over her. Pongo was a little way behind, looking after Whoopsie, as usual. She loved the idea of crawling all over Ma.

On the other side of Ma, Da was resting. the others would never climb over him, and had walked round his feet. But Whoopsie hadn't seen this. She climbed on to Da's tummy as well. It was round and bouncy, and she began to bounce up and down. Da just smiled.

Then she did a dreadful thing. She picked
up her fist and bashed Da's big shiny nose.
That hurt, and Da turned his head to one

side. When gorillas do that it means they are very cross, although Da was only doing it to protect his nose. But Whoopsie was horrified, and scampered back to Pongo.

'Da's cross with me,' she sobbed.

Pongo held out his arms and gave her a hug. Whoopsie was crying. 'Da's never been cross with me before,' she said.

'Well,' Pongo said. 'It hurts having your nose bashed. I don't think he's cross, he's just hurt. You bash your nose gently and you'll see.'

Whoopsie picked up her little fist and banged her nose hard.

'Oooh,' she howled. 'It does hurt.'

'You silly thing,' Pongo said. 'You didn't have to bang it as hard as that. But now you know why Da turned his head, don't you?'

'Yes,' Whoopsie sniffed.

'Well,' Pongo said, 'let's go and find a present for Da, to show you're sorry. Come on. I know what he'll like.'

A few minutes later Da felt a tug on his arm. There was Whoopsie with a piece of bamboo in her hand. 'It's a sorry present, Da,' she said. 'I didn't mean to hurt you.'

'I know,' Da said. 'this is a lovely piece of bamboo. Thank you, Whoopsie.'

'You're not cross any more?' Whoopsie said.

'Of course not,' Da said, and he put his arm round her. 'Now you go to Ma and have a nice drink of milk.'

And that's what Whoopsie did.

Sou'westers

A day or two later Whoopsie went running to her mother.

'Ma,' she said. 'The rain has pebbles in it.'

Ma laughed. 'It's hail,' she said. 'Little pieces of ice falling from the sky.'

'Ice?' Whoopsie said.

'Frozen water,' Ma said. 'Anyway, it's hard. And it hurts, doesn't it? We must get under the trees, I expect that's where Da will take us. Yes, look, there he is. He's beckoning to us.'

It was a heavy hailstorm. Gorillas hate getting wet and Da took them under some trees as quickly as he could. But poor little Whoopsie found that the pebbles were hurting her head.

'Come on,' Ma said. 'Get under my tummy.'

That's where Pongo and Zambi saw her: crouching under Ma's tummy.

'Poor little thing,' Pongo said. 'Her fur isn't as strong as ours yet.'

'Look,' Zambi said. 'The creeper's got a special covering on his head.'

The man was with them as usual and, of course, he was wearing a sou'wester. Pongo looked at him for a moment then he said to

Zambi, 'We must get something like that for Whoopsie. And for ourselves, come on.'

They went further into the forest and hunted for some head coverings. It was Zambi who found them. He picked one up and put it on his head. It was a plant with a sort of round crown of thick leaves with a flower in the middle.

'Oh, you do look pretty!' Pongo said when he saw him. 'But does it keep the hail off?'

'Yes,' Zambi said. 'I can't feel a thing. It's marvellous.'

Pongo picked one and put it on his head. 'You're right,' he said. 'Come on, let's pick some more for the others.'

They were soon back under the tree wearing their pretty hats. They had one for Whoopsie and one for Ma. Pongo put a hand out to Whoopsie and drew her towards him. He put the hat on her head while Ma put hers on. Soon all the gorillas were wearing pretty hats. Pongo and Zambi showed them where to find them. Da laughed and laughed at his troop but he got a pretty hat, too. Who cared about hailstorms now? Whoopsie was still kneeling under Ma's tummy because the hail hurt her all over, but she had noticed something.

'Ma,' she said, tugging at her mother's arm. 'Everybody's standing up like the creeper.'

'Yes,' Ma said. 'We always stand up in the rain. What do you think I'm doing? We don't get so wet like this.'

'Well, I must, too, then,' said Whoopsie.

'No, you're too little to stand up yet,' said Ma. 'You just stay where you are.'

But just then Pongo came past and

Whoopsie called to him, 'Teach me to stand up, Pongo.'

Zambi turned to Pongo and laughed. 'You have two new jobs,' he said. 'You seem to be more of a father than a brother to that baby.'

'No, just a teacher,' Pongo said. 'And you'll have to be one too today, because it'll need two of us to hold her up, one each side. Come on.'

So that's what they did. Whoopsie stood between them on her hind feet and they pulled

her along and taught her to walk. The hail
stopped and turned to rain, but Whoopsie still
went on with her walking lesson.

'Pull me faster,' she said suddenly. 'I
think I can run.'

She could too. Pongo and Zambi ran along beside her holding her hands. Gorillas hate rain but they forgot about it, they were so busy. Suddenly Whoopsie said, 'Take me to Da. I want to show Da I can run. I'm a big girl now.'

Pongo looked at Zambi. 'I wish she were a big bigger,' he said, 'My back feels as if it's coming in half.'

'So does mine,' said Zambi. 'But come on, let's take her to the Big Boss to show off, and perhaps she'll give up.'

When they got near to Da she said, 'Now let go, both of you.'

'You'll fall over,' Pongo said.

'No, I won't,' said Whoopsie. 'Now, let go.'

They did so and Whoopsie ran to Da with her hat over one ear. Da had been watching the walking and running lesson, but he pretended to be very surprised.

'Well, you are growing up,' he said, scooping her up. 'But now you must stop for a bit or you'll be worn out. I can see that poor Pongo and Zambi are.'

They were stretching and groaning with their pretty hats askew. Da put Whoopsie on Ma's back.

'I'm hungry,' she said.

'Come on, it's stopped raining, we'll go and find something to eat,' Ma said.

Which is exactly what they did.

Rescue

Zambi was complaining to Pongo. 'I don't think this is much of a job, being at the back of the troop,' he said. 'Nothing ever happens. I haven't needed to bang my chest or roar or anything yet.'

'I know,' Pongo said. 'But I suppose we should be glad that nothing dangerous ever happens.'

He'd spoken too soon. Something

dangerous did happen. There wasn't a leopard or a man with a gun, but Pongo's little sister was up to her tricks again. They were coming along a path by a stream. gorillas are afraid of water so they don't go near it, but Whoopsie didn't know that and she had found a fallen tree across the stream. Ma had only taken her eyes off her for a moment but it was enough. Pongo at the back of the troop suddenly heard a cry from the middle of the stream.

'Look at me.'

'There was Whoopsie on a branch bouncing up and down. Pongo beat his chest and roared. Ma and Da had to know about this. Da came rushing back and Pongo pointed at Whoopsie.

'Oh, my goodness,' Da said. 'Come back, Whoopsie. Come back.'

Whoopsie liked it in the middle of the stream so she pretended not to understand what Da was saying. 'I'll have to fetch her,' Da said.

'No,' said Ma. 'You're much too heavy for that little tree.'

'I'll fetch her,' Pongo said. 'I'm much lighter than Da. I can get across the stream further up and chase Whoopsie back. She'll come if I make a game of it.'

Pongo hurried along the path. He was quite right, it was narrower further up and there were stepping stones. It wasn't very deep either. He went carefully across the stepping stones and then ran along the bank to the other end of the tree Whoopsie was on. It was a bit thin this end and he was afraid it might not take his weight, but he crawled along very carefully and when he was quite sure that he could balance he called out to Whoopsie, 'I'm coming for you.'

Whoopsie turned round. 'Pongo,' she said. 'How did you get over there? Are you coming to play with me. Come and see what I've found. There are some funny things going under the tree, they're going very fast; silvery things.'

'Fish,' Pongo said. 'And I can go very fast, too, and I'm coming after you. I'm a big fish and I'm going to gobble you up.'

And he began to crawl as fast as he could across the tree.

'You can't catch me,' Whoopsie said. She liked chasing games. She began to crawl as fast as she could towards the bank.

'I hope she won't come too fast and fall in,' Ma said.

'I don't think she will,' said Da. 'she has
more sense than she seems to have. Anyway,
Pongo's there. He'll fish her out if he has to.'

The chase went on. Pongo crawled as
fast as he could while Whoopsie crawled
and looked round and crawled
and looked round to get
away from Pongo.

All the gorillas were standing along
the bank watching.

Pongo's game worked. In a few minutes
Whoopsie was near the bank. Da reached out
his great hand and grabbed her.

'Put me down,' Whoopsie yelled. 'Pongo will catch me.'

'Yes, do put her down,' Ma said. 'This is a chasing game. Pongo knows what he's doing.'

So Da let Whoopsie run away and climb a creeper while Pongo crawled the last bit across the tree. He grinned at Da.

'Panic over,' he said. 'But oh, that sister of mine. She's more trouble than all the rest of you put together.'

'You're telling me,' said Da. 'But thank you, Pongo, that tree would never have taken my weight.'

Pongo saw that Da was a bit disappointed that he hadn't been able to do it himself. So he said, 'Da, let's move the tree so she can't do it again. I can't lift it but I expect you can.'

Da went to the tree and with one big

heave moved it sideways. Then with a second
heave he threw it out into the stream.

'Oh, good,' said Ma, 'Now she won't be
able to reach it.'

'I'd better go on with the chase, I suppose,'
Pongo said. 'Let's hope the creeper will take
the weight of both of us.'

But he didn't have to bother because
Whoopsie had seen what her father had done.

'Da, what have you done with my tree?
You've thrown it away.'

'Yes,' Da said. 'I like throwing trees
about. It gives me an appetite for breakfast.
Come on. We'll go and find some.'

And he put Whoopsie on Ma's back and
went on in front of the troop. Pongo was
waiting to come along at the back with Zambi.

'My feet are wet,' he complained to

Zambi. 'I hate wet feet.'

Zambi laughed. 'Well, you shouldn't go paddling before breakfast,' he said.

'It was those stepping stones, said Pongo.

'Oh well,' said Zambi. 'You're a brother and brothers have to get used to wet feet.'

'Not this one,' Pongo said. 'I shan't rescue her again.'

But of course he didn't mean it and Zambi knew that. A bit later on when they were eating Da came up to Pongo.

'I want to thank you, Pongo,' he said. 'I don't know what I'd do without you.'

'Well, I don't know what we'd do without you,' Pongo said. 'I can't throw trees about like that. Whoopsie would have been in the middle of the stream again by now if you hadn't moved it. She is a little monkey!'

Da laughed and laughed. 'You're quite right there, son,' he said. 'Quite right.'

The hunter

A few days later they were back in the part of the forest they remembered well. They were eating when Zambi came up to Pongo.

'I saw the creeper go,' he said. 'He's left the troop.'

Pongo laughed. 'No,' he said, 'he's probably just gone back to his nest. You know, that wooden one. He lives near here.'

'Oh, yes,' Zambi said, and he was soon

back eating again.

They were just going off to play when
Ma came rushing towards them.

'Have you seen Whoopsie?' she said. 'I
can't find her anywhere.'

They looked for her for a while and then
Pongo said to Zambi, 'I bet I know where
she is. You know how nosey she is now. She
might have followed the man to see where
he was going.'

'Oh, yes,' Zambi said. 'You're probably
right.'

'We'll go and tell Ma and Da where
we're going,' said Pzongo. 'We'll have to go
and fetch her. It's quite a long way, though;
I don't expect she's all the way there yet.'

'We'll go on ahead, Zambi and I,' Pongo
said to Ma and Da, so they began to hurry

through the forest towards the clearing where the man's nest was. They found Whoopsie up a tree.

'Pongo,' she called. 'Look, there's another man now.'

Pongo looked. Whoopsie was right. There was a new box on wheels and there were two men coming out of the nest, the creeper with his white head and a smaller man, but big, like Da. But Pongo saw something else. The second man had a gun on his arm.

'Quick,' he said to Zambi. 'Go and tell Da. I'll get Whoopsie.'

Zambi began to argue. 'Da's coming,' he said.

'Do what you're told,' said Pongo. 'We may need Da. You know what guns can do.'

Zambi went off. But the damage was

done. Whoopsie had climbed down the tree and run towards the men. She didn't know about guns. Pongo didn't know what to do for a second. Should he beat his chest and roar? But then he heard Ma and Da behind him. So he ran straight out after Whoopsie. It was all over in a moment. There was a loud bang. Pongo threw himself on top of Whoopsie. He looked up to see that their man had knocked the gun out of the hunter's hands onto the ground. Ma and Da had reached the edge of the forest and had seen it too and they saw the hunter leap onto their man who was lying on the gun.

'Take them back,' Da said to Ma. 'That old man can't do much more.'

And then he charged with an enormous roar. The hunter looked up and saw the great ape coming at him. He couldn't reach the gun. He just turned and ran towards the box on wheels. The Big Boss chased him and took a big bite out of the seat of his trousers. The hunter yelled as he got into his car and drove away with a screech of tyres. The Big Boss turned round. Their man was limping slowly back into his nest carrying the hunter's gun.

Da wanted to thank him but he didn't know how to. What that man needs is a rest, he thought, and I'll leave him to it. He went back towards the forest. Pongo ran to meet him.

'Da,' he said. 'You attacked that hunter. You told me that gorillas never attack man.'

'They do if men attack their young,' Da said. 'He was trying to shoot you. Anyway, that bite won't kill him, it will only hurt him.

But he'll be back with some friends. We must get up into the mountains quickly.'

'But what about the creeper?' said Pongo. 'He saved my life. I ought to thank him.'

'That old man just needs a good sleep,' said Da. 'He's feeling his age like me and there's no point in him saving your life if you stay down here and lost it. Now come on. We'll catch up the others, and have a rest and some food. Then we'll start up into the mountains.'

On the way back Pongo said to Da, 'Whoopsie shouldn't have run out like that, should she? She has a lot to learn.'

'Well,' Da said, 'the only man she has met is the creeper who is a nice man. She didn't know about the other kind. I think she was frightened by the bang. She'll have to learn like you that there are nice men and nasty men. And you have to find out which they are before you go near them.'

When they reached the others Whoopsie was having milk from Ma because it made her feel better. 'She was very frightened,' Ma said.

'Good,' said Da. 'Now she'll be much safer. She won't always have a nice man like the creeper around to save her. Or Pongo.'

'Yes, she will,' Pongo said. 'I'll stay with the troop, Da.'

Ma looked at Da, who couldn't speak.

'I told you he would,' she said. 'Pongo knows he's needed.'

Later on when Pongo and Zambi were coming up at the back of the troop Zambi said to Pongo, 'Did you see the Big Boss when he charged? He had all his hair standing on end and he looked twice as big as he is.'

'Yes,' Pongo said. 'It was to frighten the hunter.'

'I noticed something else, too,' Zambi said. 'The Big Boss is turning silver all over. It's not just his back now. His chest and everything's silver.'

'Of course it is,' said Pongo. 'He's not getting any younger. That's why he needs us. that's something I wanted to ask you about, Zambi. I'm going to stay with the troop to help Da because he's getting older. Will you stay too and help me?'

'Yes,' Zambi said. 'I don't want to go and start a troop of my own. I want to stay with you and my friends here.'

'Good!' Pongo said.

A bit later on Da pulled up and they all

settled down to eat. Whoopsie stayed very close to Ma at this time. She wasn't likely to go wandering off by herself for a long time. Before they settled down for the night Da said, 'Now we're going to go to bed early. Sleep well, because we're going a long way up into the mountains tomorrow, where we'll be quite safe from men with guns. They don't go up there.'

So they bedded down and slept soundly.

Up

They kept climbing all the next day, stopping to eat and sleep and play as usual, but on the second day they found themselves at the foot of a very bare rocky bit of mountain. Da called them all together. 'Now,' he said. 'We're all going to climb up here. It's quite flat and safe at the top and there's plenty of food but this bit will be hard for some of you. But I've never seen a man up there.'

'Not even a good one,' Whoopsie said.

'No, I haven't seen any sort of man, good or bad, who can climb up this. But we can. Now, I want everyone to go up in the front except Zambi and Pongo and me. We'll stay at the back to help anyone who gets stuck. Just yell and one of us will come over and help you. The main thing is use your eyes. See where you can put your hands and feet. Now, off you go. Just call for help if you get frightened or stuck. We won't be far behind.'

'It is difficult,' Zambi said to Pongo as they started to climb. 'The rock's so slippery.'

'I suppose that's what keeps the men away,' Pongo said. 'That's why Da's brought us here. He knows what he's doing.'

It was strange. The youngsters found it easier than the older ones because they were lighter and more nimble and they hadn't got the weight to lift. But, of course, Whoopsie, who was still only a baby, got stuck two or three times. Every time she called, Da went to help her. But the third time he gave her a lecture.

'Now, Whoopsie,' he said. 'It's not clever to find the hardest way up. Look for the easiest way.'

'I didn't know it was going to be hard,' she said.

'No, of course you didn't,' Da said. 'You've never climbed a mountain like this before. You're the youngest. But this is a good mountain. Put your feet on my shoulders and reach up and you'll be able to get free.'

'I'm frightened,' she said.

'You've no need to be frightened when I'm here,' Da said. 'Hang on to my head, put your feet on my shoulders and then pull yourself up. 'It's quite easy the next bit of the way. And I'll catch you if you fall. But you won't.'

Whoopsie was soon safe.

'Stay near Ma from now on,' Da said. 'She knows what she's doing. I don't want to see you stuck again.'

Whoopsie was learning. She didn't get stuck again. But – oh dear! – the Big Boss was stuck. He had been so busy helping Whoopsie that he hadn't noticed that there were no hand-holds for him. He had to call Pongo.

'The old buffer's stuck!' Da said.

Pongo grinned. 'Not for long,' he said. 'Pongo's coming to help. Though how he's going to I don't know. You can't stand on my shoulders; I can't take your weight. I know,

I'll climb up and see if that tree is strong enough for me to hang on to.'

He climbed up and it was firm and strong. He looked over the edge of the cliff to Da.

'Now,' he said. 'I'm going to wrap my arms round the tree and make myself into a creeper, and you're to climb up using my legs like a creeper.'

'Are you sure?' asked Da.

'Of course I'm sure,' said Pongo, which was a bit of a whopper, but it was the only way he could think of to help Da. 'Now I'll yell when I've got my arms round the tree,' Pongo said. 'All right?'

'All right,' Da said.

So Pongo wrapped himself round the tree as firmly as he could.

'Come on,' he said.

Da pulled himself up as Pongo had told him, taking as much weight as he could on one arm and hanging onto Pongo with the other. He got free.

'Thank you, Pongo,' Da said when he reached him.

Pongo unwrapped his arms from the tree.

'How are you feeling?' asked Da.

'I think I've been pulled in half,' Pongo said.

But he stood up and he was quite all right. They climbed the rest of the way together.

Da said to Pongo, 'I'm getting too old for this lark, I think you'll have to be the leader of the troop now.'

'No,' Pongo said, 'I'm much too young. I

don't look like the leader of the troop. You'll have to wait until I've got a silver back and look like a leader. And I don't know as much as you do, so you'll have to wait until I know as much as a leader. You've got lots to teach me. Will you do that, Da?'

'Yes, son, but I'm getting old. I've never got stuck on a mountain before.'

'All right,' Pongo said. 'You're too old and I'm too young, but we can work together. Zambi will help, too. I've talked to him about it, and he wants to stay with the troop.'

'Well, when you've got a silver back you can be the leader of the troop – the Big Boss. And I'll go at the back with Zambi.'

'That won't be for a long time yet,' Pongo said.

They soon found some forest at the top of

the mountain which had plenty of food and
they were happy there for a long time. One
day Da had a lovely surprise. Whoopsie came
running to him.

'Da,' she said. 'I've been riding on Pongo's
back and he's got three white hairs like you.
That means he's growing up, doesn't it?'

'Yes,' Da said. 'It does, and that means
all our troubles will soon be over!'

The Penguin Who Wanted to Find Out

JILL TOMLINSON

Pictures by Paul Howard

EGMONT

Contents

It is cold

Otto was a penguin chick. He lived on his
father's feet at the bottom of the world.
That's what Leo said, anyway, that they
lived at the bottom of the world. Leo was
another penguin chick and he lived on *his*
father's feet. That is how Otto met him.

Their fathers Claudius and Nero were friends and when they stopped to talk to each other, beak to beak, Otto and Leo were almost beak to beak too. They had to shout a bit because Claudius and Nero were rather fat, like all the other penguins, so their tummies kept Otto and Leo rather far apart.

'How do you know we're at the bottom of the world?' Otto yelled across to Leo one morning.

'Your father told my father,' said Leo. 'Your father knows everything.'

'What?' yelled Otto.

'Your father knows everything,' Leo squealed back. 'Everyone goes to Claudius when they want to know anything.'

'I know that,' Otto complained bitterly. 'I can never get a word in!'

'What are you two bellowing about down there?' said a deep voice above their heads.

'Oh, Dad, there are so many things I want to know about and you never even talk to me,' Otto shouted, looking up.

A beak came down and Otto looked into Claudius's face for the first time.

'I hadn't realized how grown up you are now, Otto. I'm not your father, by the way. Call me Claudius, not Dad.'

'Why aren't you my father?'

'Because I found you in the snow when you were an egg and decided to look after you and keep you warm until you could look after yourself.'

'Didn't my own father want me then?'

'Oh, it wasn't that at all. You probably rolled off his feet when he wasn't looking. Very rolly things, eggs are. Anyway, you're all right now. You've got me.'

Otto was worried. 'But I might have fallen off,' he said.

'Fallen off what?'

'The world. Leo said this is the bottom of the world.'

'Well, it is. Antarctica it's called, the South Pole. But you won't fall off.'

'Why not?'

'Because I say so. What else do you want to ask me?'

'What am I?'

'A penguin. An emperor penguin.'

'I know that. I mean what is a penguin?'

'A bird. Now we'll have to stop talking and join the huddle of penguins, because the wind is getting up and it will be very cold soon.'

'Soon!' squeaked Otto. 'It's cold all the time!'

'It will feel even colder if you don't join the other penguins. Come on.'

Claudius began to shuffle across the ice towards the other penguins who were already huddling together to keep warm.

'Aren't there a lot of us?' Otto yelled up to Claudius.

'That's good,' Claudius boomed back at

the chick on his feet. 'The more there are,
the warmer we'll be. Now keep your beak
shut and snuggle as close as you can to me.
There's a real blizzard coming.'

Otto did what he was told but it was very
difficult to keep his beak shut. He wanted to

know what a blizzard was.

He soon found out. The wind got stronger
and stronger and it felt colder and colder.
Snow was driven at them harder and harder.
They pressed closer and closer together to
keep warm.

Soon they were too close. Otto had to open his beak: 'Claudius! Claudius! I'm getting squashed.'

He couldn't see Claudius's head because the snow blotted it out, but a voice came back through the howl of the wind.

'It's all right, Otto, get under that feathery flap below my tummy. That will protect you. Now, keep your beak shut until I say you can open it.'

Otto squeezed as hard as he could under Claudius's tummy away from the back of the penguin in front and those pressing in from each side. He had never been so cold. He thought that the snow and the wind would go on for ever. But they didn't: the wind died down and the penguins began to move apart. When he had room to bend his head

Claudius called down to Otto: 'Otto, Otto, are you all right?'

Otto stirred and he said feebly, 'Mmm, mmm, mmmm.'

Claudius was worried. 'What's the matter with you? Speak up!'

'MMM, MMM, MMM,' Otto squeaked as loudly as he could.

Claudius was puzzled. He bent down and looked closely at Otto.

'Are you all right?'

'MMMMM.'

Claudius began to laugh.

'I see. It's all my fault. You can open your beak now.'

'Oh, thank goodness,' said Otto, gasping with relief. 'It's very difficult talking with your beak shut.'

'It must be,' Claudius said. 'Anyway, did you keep warm?'

'No, I didn't. I'm cold. I don't like being cold.'

'I don't expect you to like it. You'll just have to get used to it, because we live in a cold place.'

'Can't we live somewhere else?'

'No.'

Claudius wasn't worried about Otto any more. People only complain when they are feeling better.

'I don't think I'll ever get used to being so cold,' said Otto.

'You will. I'll help you keep warm while you're little, and when you grow up you'll be covered in blubber like me. That helps a lot.'

Otto looked up at Claudius.

'Will I really be as fat as you?'

'Yes, all grown-up penguins are fat.'

'Coo,' said Otto. 'Oh well, I suppose I'll get used to it.'

The first chick

'What are you doing?' Claudius complained one morning. 'If you bounce on my feet any more you'll plant me in the snow and I'll never move again. And stop waving your flippers about like that. It feels like a blizzard blowing up there.'

Otto didn't stop. 'I'm trying to fly,' he shouted. 'You said I'm a bird. Birds fly, don't they?'

'Penguins don't fly,' Claudius said. 'Now stop jumping on my feet and I'll tell you what penguins do.'

Otto stopped. He was getting tired anyway. 'What do penguins do?' he asked, a little breathlessly.

'They swim. That's like flying in the sea. They're very good at it too.'

Otto looked up at Claudius.

'I want to fly up high like that bird up there. It's going round and round in the sky, and I want to do that.'

'Well you can't, so don't start bouncing again. Anyway, what bird?' Claudius was looking up. 'Oh my goodness, a skua. Now stay close to me, Otto. Nasty things, skuas. They like chicks.'

Otto was puzzled. 'Are you nasty then,

Claudius?'

'Am I . . .? Oh I see! I like chicks, but not for dinner. A skua will dive down from the sky and steal a nice juicy penguin chick for its next meal. That's why you mustn't wander off by yourself.'

'I didn't know I could wander off by myself,' Otto said. 'I'm stuck on your feet.'

'Not for ever, thank goodness,' Claudius said, shifting his poor trampled toes. 'You're nearly big enough to walk beside me now, and soon you'll have all the other chicks to play with.'

'What other chicks?' Otto said. 'There's only Leo and me.'

'There are lots of other chicks now, you'll find. You and Leo were the first chicks to hatch, but you aren't the only ones. When that skua has gone I'll take you round and you'll see what a lot of you there are.'

Claudius was right. All the grown-ups seemed to be shuffling around with chicks on their feet. Every round white tummy had a little head peeping out under it. Nearly every round white tummy, that is, because Otto was waddling along beside Claudius. Leo couldn't believe his eyes when he saw Otto coming towards him.

'Otto!' He shouted up at Nero. 'Dad, look! Otto's walking by himself.'

'Oh yes,' said Nero. 'You can go and meet him if you like.'

'Me?' Leo said. 'By myself?'

'Yes, go on. You're big enough now.'

Leo looked at the ice all around him. He wasn't at all sure that he wanted to leave the shelter of Nero's nice warm feet.

'Won't my feet get cold?'

'Not very,' said a voice quite near him. It was Otto. 'Come on, Leo. We're the first chicks. That's very special. We have to show all the little ones what to do.'

'I don't *know* what to do,' said Leo. 'Anyway, you may be the first chick but I'm only the second. I'm not at all sure that I'm ready yet.'

Nero was sure. He tipped Leo on to the ice and walked across to talk to Claudius. Leo squeaked, picked himself up and ran after Nero, but Otto headed him off.

'Catch me!' he
called, running a little
way. 'I bet you can't.'
Leo couldn't resist
that, so a chase
began. It lasted a
long time. Claudius
and Nero watched the two
downy little chicks tumbling about in the
snow having a wonderful time.

'Let's join them,' Claudius said suddenly.

'Join them?' Nero said. 'I'm too old for that sort of fun and games.'

'No, you're not,' Claudius said. 'It's going to be the easiest way to collect them up. Come on, I bet you can't catch me.'

So then there were four of them in the game and they had a lot of fun. One of the new chicks wanted to join in but his father wouldn't let him.

'No, not yet. When you're a bit older you can.'

The new chick was very disappointed, but a little later Claudius and Nero went past with Otto and Leo back on their feet. Otto saw the new little chick watching and called out, 'Hello. What's your name?'

'Gusto. Can I play with you next time?'

'You can play with us when your dad says you can. You're not big enough yet.'

'I'm not very big outside, but I'm *enormous* inside,' Gusto said.

Claudius laughed above Otto's head as they moved on.

'You're going to have trouble with that one, Otto,' he said.

'I am?' Otto said. 'He has a father, hasn't he? I won't have to look after him.'

'You will,' Claudius said. 'You're the first chick so you'll have to look after the whole clutch.'

'You mean all of them?'

Otto looked around slowly. There were penguins as far as he could see and nearly all of them had chicks or eggs on their feet.

'No, just your own gang around here. They'll keep you busy, though.'

They did. A few days later Otto and Leo had lots of new friends. When it was warm enough they tumbled from their fathers' feet and played together. The very little ones like Gusto just didn't understand that they must stay together to be safe. Otto, watching the skuas circling hopefully above them, had to keep rounding them up.

'Gusto!' he was always having to yell.

'Come back, you must stay close to me.'

'Why?' said Gusto. 'I only want to see what's over there.'

'Because I say so. You'll end up as a skua's dinner if you wander round by yourself. We must all stay together to be safe. Come on.'

'Oh, all right,' Gusto said, wandering back into the group. 'But I can look after myself. You are *bossy*, Otto.'

Nero and all the other fathers were very glad that Otto was bossy. They didn't have to worry about their chicks very much.

'Your Otto looks after them all beautifully,' one said to Claudius. 'You must be very proud, Claudius.'

Claudius *was* very proud. Otto didn't know it, though. He came back to Claudius one night and called up to him.

'Claudius, am I bossy?'

'Yes,' said Claudius. 'Very.'

'Oh dear,' Otto said. 'They keep telling me I am, but how else can I keep them safe?'

'How else?' Claudius said. 'You be bossy. First chicks always have to be bossy. You'll soon learn that.'

Penguins look after each other

Claudius blinked the sleep from his eyes and pointed his beak towards the voice at his feet.

'Yes, Otto, what is it?'

'I have a very funny feeling in my tummy. An asking sort of feeling. What is it?'

'You're hungry, I expect.'

'What's hungry?'

'An asking feeling in your tummy. I've got it too. We need something to eat. We'll have to go and see if the ladies are back from the sea.'

'The ladies?'

'Yes, they've been eating fish and things in the sea so that they can feed you chicks. I'll find you a nice aunty and she'll feed you with shrimp soup. It's delicious. You'll like that, and that empty feeling will go away for a bit.'

'Will you have some too, Claudius?'

'Well, no. I shall have to say goodbye to you and go off to the sea to find lots of food. I've had nothing to eat all winter and I'm very hungry.'

'You mean you'll go away without me?'

'Yes, Otto. You're not big enough to come

to the sea yet.'

Otto was horrified. 'You wouldn't leave me, Claudius. I need you.'

'No you don't. I'll find a nice aunty to look after you. She'll be just as good as me, and you'll still have me inside. That's the important place to have a good dad – inside.'

'But I want you *outside* where I can see you. Oh, don't leave me, Claudius.'

Poor Otto was shattered. But Claudius began to lead him towards the sea and the journey was so interesting that Otto began to forget how miserable he was. He had never been away from the rookery of penguins before. The white ice stretched round them as far as he could see.

'The bottom of the world is very big,' he said at last.

'Yes, Antarctica is very big,' Claudius said. 'Look, over there. A Weddell seal and her pup.'

Otto looked. A huge fat creature lay on the ice with a smaller one cuddled up to her.

'Marvellous divers, seals are,' Claudius said. 'They can dive much deeper than us.'

'Dive?' Otto asked.

'Go a very long way down into the water,' explained Claudius. 'You'll see them go past you when *you're* in the sea.'

'What do they do when there's a blizzard?' Otto said. 'There don't seem to be any others around to huddle with.'

'No, they just have to hope they're fat enough to keep warm. They're almost solid blubber so they're usually all right.'

'The chick . . . the pup, I mean, has a

nice face,' Otto said, as they got nearer to the seals. 'What are those hairy bits on his face?'

'Whiskers,' Claudius said. 'All seals have whiskers. Now look carefully at those seals because they're Weddell seals and they look a bit like leopard seals. You must learn never to get them mixed up.'

'Why?' asked Otto. 'Aren't leopard seals nice?'

'No, not nice at all. They eat penguins. Weddell seals only eat fish and things and they're quite harmless. But you must watch out for leopard seals when you first go to sea. Weddells have smaller heads and in time you will learn the difference, but at first it's best to keep away from all spotted seals.'

Otto suddenly stopped dead.

'Claudius, the ice is moving!' he shouted.

'Look at it!'

'That's the sea,' Claudius said. 'And look, there's someone coming to meet us. One of the ladies, I expect.'

It was. She kept shaking herself to get rid of the water on her feathers before it turned to ice. As she came nearer to them Claudius suddenly said, 'It's Anna. She'll make a good aunty for you.'

Otto moved and hid himself behind Claudius's back.

'I don't want an aunty. I want to keep my dad.'

Claudius turned round and rubbed the top of Otto's head with his beak.

'Sorry, Otto,' he said. 'But you are an emperor penguin and emperor penguins have to get used to lots of different mothers and fathers when they are growing up.'

Otto looked up at Claudius. 'But the seal pup had someone all to himself. I want you all to myself.'

'Of course you do, but you have a nice huddle of friends to belong to. That seal pup hasn't got anything like that. Penguins look after each other. Will you look after me?'

Otto gaped at him.

'How? You're going away.'

'Will you let me go and feed myself? I'm starving. My asking feeling inside really hurts. You can help me by letting me go.'

Otto didn't know what to say. But he knew what he had to do. He waddled round to the front of Claudius again and looked towards Anna. 'She's not bad, I suppose,' he agreed at last.

Claudius tapped Otto's head with his beak.

'Thank you,' he said. Then he called out, 'Anna, I have a hungry chick here waiting for you.'

Anna began to waddle even faster towards them.

'Open your beak, Otto,' Claudius said.

'I don't feel like talking.'

'Not to talk. So that Anna can feed you,' laughed Claudius. 'Anna, this is Otto. He's our first chick this year.'

'Oh, I shall be very proud to be *his* aunty then. Hello, Otto. You must be very hungry. Open your beak and I'll give you some fish soup.'

It was good. In a few minutes the empty feeling in Otto's tummy had nearly gone. Anna moved back, taking her beak out of Otto's.

'More,' Otto said. 'Please, Anna.'

'Come on then,' Anna said. 'I'm glad you like what I've brought you.'

So Otto had his first meal.

Claudius went down to the sea to have *his* first meal of the winter when he saw that Otto was all right. He knew that Anna would look after him well.

When Otto was quite full he stood back from his new aunty and saw that Claudius had gone. The ice stretched around them white and empty. Otto's head drooped. No more Claudius. How could he live without Claudius? Anna understood.

'Come on, Otto,' she said. 'Claudius will soon be full too. Will you show me the way home?'

Otto turned round slowly and began to lead the way. What had Claudius said to him? Penguins help each other. And he was a penguin. He would have to get used to it!

The last chick

Otto was so busy during the next few days that he didn't have much time to miss Claudius. As the ladies came back from the sea to feed the chicks all the fathers disappeared one by one to feed themselves. Otto had to look after all his huddle. Often he had to huddle the chicks together when the grown-ups were still walking about. They had enough blubber to keep them warm but the chicks hadn't yet.

When they began to feel the cold Otto and Leo collected all the chicks together in a tight huddle, the little ones in the centre where it was warmest. When he had finished making the very first chick huddle of this kind, Otto noticed a chick standing all by himself some way away, looking out to sea.

'Oh dear,' he said to Leo. 'Look, we've left someone out. I must go and fetch him.'

Leo looked across at the chick.

'Oh yes, that's Alex. He was the last chick to hatch so he's only a baby. We must keep him warm.'

Otto hurried off. As he got nearer to the chick he could see that Leo was right. Alex was just a baby. He wasn't really big enough to be off his father's feet. He looked so cold and miserable standing there that Otto knew he must get him into the huddle quickly.

'Where's Daddy?' wailed Alex, as soon as Otto reached him. 'I want my father.'

'I expect he was hungry,' Otto said. 'Aren't you hungry?'

'That's what that lady penguin asked me,' Alex said. 'I didn't know what she meant, so she went away. What's hungry?'

Otto looked at him. 'It's an asking feeling inside, but I don't expect you have it yet. So you haven't got an aunty?'

'No, I haven't got anybody at all.'

Otto felt very fatherly. 'My name is Otto,' he said. 'You stay close to me and I'll look after you. Come on, we must get back to our huddle.'

Alex waddled along beside Otto for a few yards and then he stopped.

'Otto!' he wailed. Otto stopped too.

'What's the matter?'

'You're not a proper father at all,' Alex said. 'Your feet aren't big enough.'

Otto looked down at his feet. Alex was quite right.

'No, I can't give you a ride yet,' he said. 'But perhaps my feet will grow in the warmth of the huddle, so let's hurry there. Come on, run.'

So Otto and Alex arrived at the huddle at last, Otto pushing the baby in front of him for the last little bit. He tried to push him to the centre of the huddle but Alex wouldn't leave him.

'I want to stay with you, Otto,' he said, standing firmly on Otto's feet. 'You can be my father now.'

Gusto was standing near them and he
began to screech with laughter.

'Old bossy chick has a baby,' he shouted.

'When you're quite finished, cheeky
chick, you can come and help me look after
him,' Otto said. 'Come on. You keep his front
warm while I keep the wind off his back.'

'Why?' said Gusto. 'I'm busy keeping
myself warm.'

'Because penguins, emperor penguins anyway, look after each other. Come on, put your tummy against his. That's right. Alex, this is Gusto. He talks an awful lot, but he's a very nice chap.'

Alex looked shyly up at Gusto. 'If you talk a lot, you must be able to tell stories? I do like stories. Please tell me a story.'

Gusto looked helplessly at Otto.

'I've never told a story. Where do I get it from?'

'Out of your head. I'm sure there are lots in yours. Just begin "Once upon a time" and carry on from there.'

So Gusto began. Soon Otto's worries about little Alex were over. He was so happy listening to Gusto's stories that he didn't even notice how cold he was. Not until it got a bit warmer and the huddle began to drift apart. Gusto was hungry so he gabbled the end of his last story and went off to find his aunty.

'Otto,' Alex wailed, 'Gusto's gone. I'm cold, horribly cold.'

'Yes, Alex, I expect you are. We live in a cold place you see. You'll get used to it.'

'Have you got used to it yet, Otto?'

'Well, no, not quite. I'm only a chick like you, you know. When we get bigger and fatter we won't feel so cold. The way to do that is to eat. Come on. I'm going to find aunty Anna.'

They found aunty Anna and Otto had a good feed. When he had finished he was very surprised to see Alex come up to Anna and say: 'Me, too.'

'What's this?' Otto said. 'I thought you weren't hungry yet?'

'I think I am now,' Alex said. 'Will you be my aunty, Anna?'

'Well, I don't know,' Anna said. '*Two* chicks to feed. I shall be worn out.'

Otto looked at her. 'Alex is the last chick around here, Anna. It means that you'll have the first and the last. That's very special.'

Anna grinned at Otto. 'All right, you've talked me into it. We'll find Alex an aunty of his own soon, but I'll feed him for the time being. Come on, little one.'

So Alex had his first meal. An enormous one.

'There won't be much left for you tomorrow, Otto,' Anna said. 'I'll have to go down to the sea again. Never mind. There'll be plenty of aunts and uncles coming to feed you all from now on.'

'You mean I'll have to get used to somebody different?' Otto asked. 'I've only just got to know you.'

'That's how it is with emperor penguins. The grown-ups go backwards and forwards to the sea to get food for you until you're big enough to go yourselves. You'll have lots of different penguins to look after you but you won't go hungry. Penguins look after each other.'

That's what Claudius said, Otto thought. But lots of different penguins to feed him! Oh well, he was a penguin. He'd get used to it.

Pup

Next day, when Otto was going down to the sea to try to find someone bringing up food, he saw something huge and fat lying on the ice: a seal. He was quite pleased at first, because it would be somebody to talk to. But as he got nearer Otto could see that the seal was spotted. What had Claudius said? 'Spotted seals might be leopard seals and they are dangerous.' This one didn't look very dangerous. He was so fat he could hardly move, and he was playing a sort of rolling game with himself. Then he saw Otto and waved a flipper. Otto thought he knew that face. He kept moving. Sure enough, it was the pup he had seen before with Claudius, but he was very much bigger now. Otto stopped a little distance away from the seal. The seal was so fat he could hardly move and even though Otto was no great mover he reckoned he could get out of the way if it were a leopard seal.

'Hello,' Otto said. 'Haven't I met you before?'

'You've passed me before. You didn't talk to me,' said the seal.

'I'm sorry,' Otto said. 'I was with Claudius and he was in a hurry. He was hungry.'

'That sounds like my mother,' said the seal. 'She's taught me to catch fish and look after myself. So now she's gone back to sea to feed herself again. She'd got terribly thin. Her bones were sticking out.'

'I can't say the same for you,' said Otto.

The seal laughed. 'No, I got fat very quickly, and as I got fatter my mother got thinner. It was all the milk I had, you see.'

'Milk?' said Otto. 'What's milk?'

'Well, it's what I was fed on,' said the seal. 'I'm a mammal, you see.'

'What's a mammal?' said Otto.

'Well, I expect you came out of an egg, didn't you, because you're a bird. Well, mammals don't. Seals are the only mammals in Antarctica. My mother told me that and she stayed with me and kept me warm and fed me on milk until I was big enough to look after myself.'

'That's what I'm doing,' said Otto. 'Waiting to be big enough to look after myself. When I am I can go to the sea, but at the moment I'm fed by the grown-up penguins who bring fish soup and squid soup and all sorts of nice things.'

'Oh, I get my own squid and fish now,' said the seal. 'I may meet you in the sea. Do penguins dive?'

'Yes. We have to to get our food,' said Otto.

'Well, I might pass you one day. My mother says that we are the best divers in the world. We can dive two thousand feet. How deep can you dive?'

'I don't know,' said Otto. 'But Claudius did tell me that Weddell seals are very good divers and can dive deeper than us. What's your name? It seems silly to know somebody and not know his name. My name's Otto.'

'I haven't got a name,' said the seal. 'My mother always called me Pup and that was it.'

'Well, can I call you Pup?' asked Otto.

'Yes, Otto, you do that,' said Pup. 'Now I want to ask you something. Have you got any teeth?'

'Teeth?' said Otto. 'No, I don't think so. What are they?'

Pup opened his mouth and showed Otto his teeth. 'I need them,' he said. 'You see, when it's very cold I come up in the sea and find ice over my head. I have to get air to breathe, so I bite and bite the ice until I've made a breathing hole.'

'Oh, I've seen those,' said Otto. 'Just holes

in the ice.'

'That's right,' said Pup. 'Well, that's what I have to have teeth for: because I have to breathe. It's hard work, though, if the ice is very thick.'

'Yes, your teeth do look as if you've been using them a lot,' said Otto. 'They're all sort of flat at the top. But then I don't know what they should look like anyway. So you've been to the sea. Is it fun?'

'Oh yes,' said Pup. 'I love it. And it's full of food. My mother taught me bit by bit how to catch shrimps and krill and squid, but now I can catch fish as well. She taught me everything I need to know. I do miss her.'

'I miss Claudius, too,' said Otto. 'He taught me all I know, but he had to go to sea to feed before I had finished growing up. You were lucky to have your mother until you'd finished growing up. Anyway, I'd better stop talking and go down to the beach. Otherwise there won't be any food left for me. All the other chicks will have got it.'

'I'll come with you,' said Pup. 'It's time I got back to the sea, too. The sea's warmer than the ice.'

'Really?' said Otto.

'Yes,' said Pup.

So they went down the beach together, although Otto had to be very patient because Pup was so fat and slow. When they got there, Pup waved a flipper and disappeared into the sea, and Otto found an aunty to feed him. On the way back to the rookery Otto thought to himself, 'I wish I were a seal.

Penguins do take a long time to grow up.
But I suppose I'll get used to it.'

Growing

Otto was always hungry these days and the grown-ups always brought food from the sea. In fact, he began to enjoy meeting all the different grown-ups. Most of them were quite ordinary, but there were some specially nice ones. Justin was one of these. Otto had gone down towards the sea to look for someone to feed him and met Justin looking for someone to feed.

'My goodness,' Justin said, 'I'm hardly out of the sea. But all right, squid soup today.'

When Otto had finished he stood back and said, 'Delicious. I like squid soup.'

'Well, you'll be able to get your own soon. You're a big chap.'

'I'm first chick,' Otto said. 'Can you tell me something? The sea is getting nearer. Why?'

'The ice is breaking up at the edge of the sea because it's getting warmer. Antarctica's made of ice so it gets smaller every summer.'

'Oh, you sound just like Claudius,' Otto said. 'He always explained everything to me like that. I do miss him. He was my first father. He *was* good.'

'Of course he was good,' Justin said. 'I trained him. He was my chick once.'

'Claudius was *your* chick?' Otto said.

'You must be old!'

'Not that old,' said Justin. 'Anyway, let's go back to the rookery. We can talk on the way.'

Otto asked all the questions that he would have asked Claudius if he had still been around as they waddled back. At last Justin said:

'I think perhaps I *am* getting old. I'm tired. I can't answer any more questions.'

'Just one, Justin, please. Just one,' Otto said.

'All right, one,' said Justin.

'I just want to know when I can toboggan,' Otto said. 'I've seen the grown-ups slide across the ice very fast on their tummies. It does look fun.'

'You'll be able to toboggan when you

have your adult feathers,' Justin said.

'When will that be?'

'That's a second question,' Justin said.
'I said one.'

He saw Otto's head droop. He moved
away but called back over his shoulder: 'Soon.'

Soon? Otto wanted to ask *how* soon, but
he knew it was no good. He would just have
to wait.

A few days later the cold wind began to
blow and Otto knew he would have to get the
smaller chicks into a warm huddle. He had
an easy way of doing this now. All he had to
do was find Gusto and send round a whisper
that Gusto was going to tell stories. Then all
the chicks would hurry over and press close
to him to hear the stories, and there was the
huddle. Gusto was chief storyteller now and

he enjoyed his job. So Otto got Gusto to stand in a sheltered place and soon there was a big huddle of small penguins round him. Then bigger ones joined in round the edge.

One of these, a rather bad-tempered chick called Nap, began to make a fuss.

'What's Gusto doing in the centre of the huddle with the babies where it's warmest? He's as big as me. He should be on the outside,' he groused.

'He's doing a job,' Leo said.

'Yes, a very important job,' Otto joined in.

'He's big enough to be on the edge like me. Hey, Gusto,' Nap yelled.

'Shut up,' said Otto quietly.

'I won't shut up,' Nap said, giving Otto a push. 'Who do you think *you* are? Do you want a fight?'

'No,' said Otto, 'emperor penguins *don't* fight, because it's important for them to stay friends and huddle together to keep warm.'

'Coward,' said Nap. 'Come on, fight!'

'No,' Otto said. 'I'm an emperor penguin.

Perhaps you're an adelie penguin. They squabble all the time. They lay their eggs in nests and even bicker over whose nest it is. We're supposed to be sensible chaps.' Otto

held his head in the air and looked at Nap
down his beak. 'Go and find an adelie
penguin to fight with or shut up.'

Nap shut up. There was sense in what
Otto said.

Leo, who was on the other side of Otto,
said, 'Where did you learn all that, Otto?'

'From Justin,' Otto said. 'I'm so glad I
met him.'

He was, too, when Alex crept up to him
after the huddle.

'Otto,' he said. 'I think I ought to tell you
about something.'

'Well, go on then,' Otto said. 'What
should you tell me about?'

'You're . . .' Alex swallowed, '. . . you're
going bald!'

Otto looked down at himself. There were

patches of down missing and thick white feathers showing through underneath.

'Yippee!' he shouted to the astonished Alex.

'Don't you mind?' Alex said.

'Mind?' said Otto. 'Going bald means I'm growing up.'

He rushed off to find Leo. Leo was second chick so he was probably shedding his down, too. He was. Soon all the older chicks had bald patches.

'We look an awful mess,' Leo said one morning. 'But it is exciting watching each other turn into proper penguins. You're getting a yellow collar, Otto, as well as black bits all down your back.'

'Am I?' Otto said. 'I wish I could see myself.'

Little Alex came up.

'I understand now,' he said to Otto. 'You are all going bald. I wish it would happen to me. I'm still fluffy all over.'

'It *will* happen to you, last chick. You'll just have to be very patient,' Otto said.

'I wish I were first chick, like you,' Alex said. 'You don't have to be patient like me.'

Otto laughed. 'Yes, I'm a very lucky chap.'

'Oh, you are silly, Alex,' Leo said. 'It takes just as long to grow up whether you hatch early or late.'

'Yes, but it must seem longer when you're the last one,' said Otto. 'Poor Alex. Never mind. At least you'll know what's coming next all the time. We haven't a clue. But I suppose we'll get used to it.'

Knowing

But this time Otto and Leo could not get
used to it. They had to know what was going
to happen next.

'We'll ask a grown-up,' said Otto. 'Come
on, it's feeding time anyway.'

So they set off towards the sea to meet
the adults coming up with food for them. Otto
found an aunt, Cathy; Leo found an uncle,
Julius. When they met again at the rookery

Otto and Leo rushed towards each other.

'What have you found out?' Otto asked.

'We'll be able to go to sea ourselves soon,' Leo said.

'When?' asked Otto.

'Julius was a fat lot of help. He just said we'd *know* when.'

'Cathy said the same,' Otto said. 'She said that when we're ready a group of us will go together. The sea is full of life and we just have to swim around and collect it for ourselves.'

'Swim?' asked Leo. 'What's that?'

'It's like flying, but in the water. We waggle our flippers. Claudius told me about it. It's what penguins are best at, swimming. I'm longing to try, but we have to wait until we've lost all our down.'

'Why?' said Leo. 'You should know. You seem to know everything.'

'Because I say so,' Otto said firmly. He had no idea. Perhaps down soaked up the water and got in the way. He'd have to find a grown-up who knew next feeding time.

The trouble was, not all adults were good at answering questions, or would try. In the end it was another chick who told him. A lady, first chick of another huddle. He met her on the edge of the rookery. She greeted him with: 'You've shed all your down. You're ready.'

Otto gaped at her. 'All of it? Really?'

She waddled all round him. 'Yes. You've got all your adult feathers. Dense oily feathers which will make you waterproof. What about me?'

Otto waddled round her.

'You've one tiny tuft of down left on your
back. Shall I peck it off for you?'

'No. Thank you, though it was kind of
you to offer. But it has to come off by itself
when it's ready – when the feathers underneath
are oily enough.'

168

'I see,' Otto said. 'What's your name?'

'Josie.'

'Oh, thank you, Josie. You must have had a good father to tell you things.'

'Yes, I did. But most of my huddle think I'm a bossy know-all.'

'Me too,' Otto said. 'It *is* nice to meet someone like you.'

So they enjoyed a good grumble about the problems of being first chick in their huddles. At last they thought they had better go back, so they parted.

'See you tomorrow, Josie, perhaps,' Otto said. 'Goodbye for now.'

'Goodbye, Otto. I've learned a lot from you.'

Otto had learned a lot too. When he bumped into Leo, Leo cried, 'You're a proper penguin, Otto – all black and white and yellow. Am I?'

Otto waddled round him.

'You only have two bits of down left and they're on your back.'

'Oh, Otto, peck 'em off,' Leo begged.

'Please, Otto.'

'No,' Otto said. 'I wouldn't be doing you a good turn at all. The feathers underneath can't be ready yet.'

'Oh, all right, Mr Know-all. I'll get someone else to peck them off.'

'No, Leo, please wait. The thing is your feathers have to get properly oily before you go in the sea. You might sink otherwise.'

'Sink? You told me that penguins are marvellous swimmers.'

'We are. When our feathers are ready. You won't have long to wait now.'

'*Wait*,' groaned Leo. 'We're always waiting for something.'

'Yes, we are. I'm having to wait for you before we go to sea. I'm not going without you.'

'Oh, Otto, you're going on waiting just for me?'

'Yes,' grinned Otto. 'I'll get used to it.'

All at sea

Otto could not get a meal next day. 'You're not a chick. You're a penguin,' the adults kept saying.

'Only just,' he cried. But nobody would feed him.

So that's what they'd meant when they'd said he would know when he was ready. They wouldn't *feed* him when he was ready, so hunger would drive him to the sea.

Soon there was quite a crowd of angry
young penguins standing at the edge of the
rookery complaining about the mean
adults, and Leo was among them.
He came waddling towards Otto.

'What do we do now?' he wailed.
'We're starving.'

'What do you think we do? Where shall we
find squid and fish and krill and all the other
things that grown-ups keep bringing us?'

'The sea!' Leo said. 'Come on,
everybody. To sea!'

He started to waddle in the right direction
but Otto shot past him on his tummy.

'Come on,' Otto cried. 'Toboggan. It's
much quicker.'

Soon they were all tobogganing, shooting
across the ice on their fat feathery fronts

propelled by their strong flippers. Their steering wasn't very good at first and there were a lot of collisions. Otto met Josie again by bumping into her.

'*Whoops* – sorry!' he said. 'Oh, Josie!'

'Yes, it's me,' said Josie. 'Isn't this fun? I've always wanted to do this.'

'Me too,' Otto said. 'The only thing is, is it all right for us to leave our huddles to look after themselves now? I feel a bit guilty.'

'Don't worry,' said Josie, pushing herself along beside him. 'It's warm enough now. They'll be all right. They'll join us soon. Forget them. Come on. Let's have a race. I'll beat you to the sea.'

She shot off in front of him and Otto was so busy chasing her that he forgot all about his chicks.

But his job wasn't quite over. When they reached the edge of the sea all the young penguins bunched together, afraid to go on. It was up to Otto and Josie and the other first chicks to go in first. There were six of them. They looked at each other. Otto was scared, but he remembered what Claudius had said: 'Penguins look after each other.'

'Come on!' he yelled, 'food!' and splashed in. He leaned forward and moved his flippers. Yes, he could swim. In fact, swimming was even faster than tobogganing. Soon he was swimming about on top of the water and calling out to Leo.

'Come on, it's easy.'

Leo and all the others were soon in, but after the joy of finding that they could swim they began to remember something.

'Well, where's the food?' one of them shouted.

'Underneath you,' replied Josie. 'We have to dive for it, like this.'

She disappeared head first. The others copied her. Otto decided that this was the best bit yet, swimming under water. It was so interesting down there.

He wasn't hungry very much longer. He met a fish, opened his beak and swallowed it. He went to the bottom and saw something moving under a rock. He grabbed its leg and pulled. Well, now he knew what a squid looked like. That went the same way as the fish.

After a few krill, he torpedoed back up to the surface. It was quite a long way up. He was just going to start swimming back to the beach when he saw Josie. She was looking up at a cliff of ice. Suddenly she dived into the water and disappeared. Perhaps she was still hungry.

But then she came up again – and *up* was the word. She leaped clean out of the water and right up the cliff.

'Be careful,' Otto shouted.

But he needn't have bothered. Josie looked down at him from the top of the cliff where she had landed and shouted, 'You can do it, Otto. My father told me about this. It's penguins' leap. You're a penguin, aren't you?'

Otto needed no more urging than that. He tried to leap, but fell back with a splash.

Josie laughed down at him. 'That's not the way!' she shouted. 'Dive a long way down and then torpedo up as fast as you can and just keep going.'

Otto did what he was told.

He found himself on top of the ice cliff near to Josie. He had landed on his feet as if he had been doing it all his life. Oh, he did feel pleased with himself. He could toboggan, he could swim, he could feed himself and now he could leap.

Josie came towards him. 'Well, Otto, do you like being a penguin?'

'I'll get used to it,' he said happily.

The Aardvark Who Wasn't Sure

JILL TOMLINSON

Pictures by Paul Howard

EGMONT

Contents

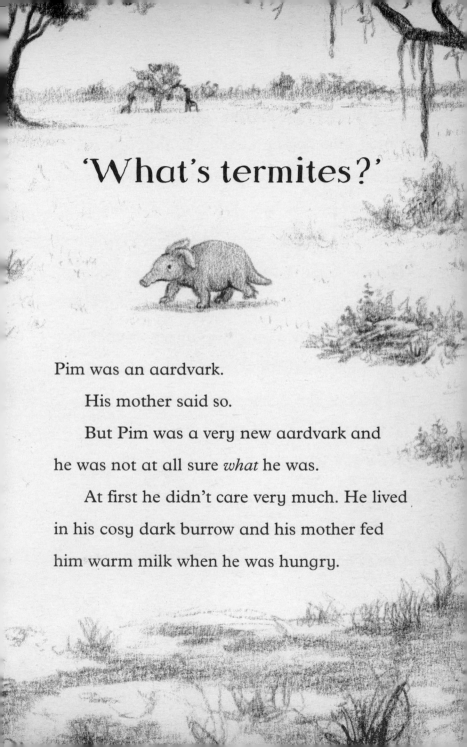

'What's termites?'

Pim was an aardvark.

His mother said so.

But Pim was a very new aardvark and he was not at all sure *what* he was.

At first he didn't care very much. He lived in his cosy dark burrow and his mother fed him warm milk when he was hungry.

Between his feeds he just slept, like most babies.

But as he grew bigger, he began to notice things. One day he woke up to find that his mother wasn't there. He had thought that she was always with him. He shuffled around the burrow looking for her but he couldn't find her. Then he found a sort of sloping tunnel. Perhaps she was up there. He began to shuffle along it. Then he heard scraping sounds. Something was coming down the tunnel towards him! He backed into the burrow just in time. His mother burst in, nearly knocking him over.

'Pim!' she said. 'You're supposed to be asleep.'

'You were supposed to be here!' shouted Pim, who had been rather frightened. 'Where have you been?'

'Where have I been? Getting food, of

course. I have to eat sometimes.'

'Food?' said Pim.

'Termites,' his mother said. 'You have milk now, but when you're bigger you'll eat termites.'

'Why?' said Pim. 'Why will I eat termites?'

'Because you're an aardvark. Aardvarks eat termites. Now, do you want your feed or are you going to ask silly questions all night?'

Pim was hungry, so he had his feed. But as soon as his tummy felt full, he asked the question that was bothering him.

'What's termites?'

'Go to sleep,' said his mother. 'You'll find out soon enough.'

'But what are they like?' Pim asked. 'I only want to know.'

'Oh dear,' said Pim's mother. 'I have a

feeling you're the kind who never stops wanting to know.'

'Well?' said Pim. 'What's termites?'

'What *are* termites,' his mother corrected him. 'Crawly things. They are very like ants. They live in big nests that we have to rip open. They're nice, termites. Soft and juicy. You'll like them.'

'Rip open their nests?' said Pim. 'How?'

'With the claws on our front feet. We're very strong, you know.'

'How do I know I'm very strong?' said Pim doubtfully.

'Because you're an aardvark. Now go to sleep.'

Pim was very sleepy and dropped off almost at once. That evening his mother had a surprise for him.

'Would you like to come with me tonight?' she asked him. 'I think it's time you saw the world outside.'

'Oh yes,' said Pim. 'Can I eat some termites?'

'Well, I don't think so,' his mother said. 'I shouldn't think you'd like them yet. But you can watch me so that you'll know what to do when you're big enough to get them yourself.'

So a little later Pim the aardvark followed his mother up the tunnel and stepped out just a little way into the African night. As far as he could see the land stretched out, flat and empty.

'The world is very big,' Pim said, moving closer to his mother.

'It is,' she said. 'Now, be very quiet and listen. We have to see if it's safe to go out.'

Pim's mother stood very still and pricked

up her long ears.

Pim copied her. At first he could hear nothing, but soon he became aware of a soft swishing noise all around them. He looked at his mother. It didn't seem to be bothering her.

'What's that?' he asked her. 'That whispering.'

'Just the grasses,' she said.

Suddenly there was a muffled roar – and then again.

'What's that?' said Pim, quivering all over.

'A lion,' she said. 'It's all right, it's a long way away. I don't think it will bother us. Now, let's see if you can run.'

Pim's mother began to move forward in a shambling gallop.

Pim didn't know how to begin. He stood transfixed for a second, unable to move.

Then he heard the lion roar again.

Pim found that he could run.

They travelled across the veldt for some way, Pim's mother lolloping gently so that Pim could keep up with her. Pim began to enjoy it. This was much more fun than staying at home in the earth burrow.

They passed a few scrubby trees. Then they came to some huge humps in the ground of all shapes and sizes. Pim's mother stopped suddenly, in front of the very biggest one.

'This will do,' she said. 'Now, watch.'

Pim watched as his mother began to tear at the side of the hump with her powerful claws. Soon she had made a gaping hole.

Then Pim saw a termite, and another and another. They came pouring out of the hole in panic. They didn't like having their

nest broken open like this. Mrs Aardvark
began to shoot out her long, sticky pink
tongue and lick them up. Tongueful after
tongueful of termites disappeared like magic.
Then she pushed her long muzzle right into
the nest, through the hole she had made, to
lick up the rest of the termites.

Pim was amazed. Although the termites
were tiny, they had very fierce faces and he
wouldn't fancy putting *his* nose right inside
one of their nests.

Still, if that's what aardvarks did, he would have to learn to do it. He put out his tongue and looked down at it. Yes, it was very long and pink and curly at the end, just like his mother's. When his mother turned round, her dinner finished, she found him sitting on his tail pulling faces. He was trying to shoot his tongue in and out, keeping his eyes on it all the time. This gave him a terrible squint.

'What are you doing?' laughed his mother.

'I am practising being an aardvark,' said Pim with dignity. He stopped and looked at his mother.

'Do you really like termites?' he said. 'They look horrible to me.'

'Delicious,' said his mother. 'That was a lovely dinner. But I expect you'd rather have some milk, wouldn't you? Come on then. Home.'

So Pim and his mother galloped home across the veldt.

Monkey business

Pim was very tired after his first outing. He slept all day and all night.

When he woke up his mother was just coming back from her night's termite hunt. Pim was furious.

'You went without me!' he shouted. 'You left me behind.'

'Yes, dear,' said his mother. 'You were fast asleep and I thought it would be best if

I left you.'

'I wanted to come. You should have waited for me.' Pim was very disappointed, which was why he was so cross.

'Aren't you hungry?' said his mother, who understood. 'Come and have your feed. Then you can go up the tunnel and sit in the sun and watch the world go by for a little while if you like.'

This seemed a very nice idea. Pim *was* hungry, very hungry. He settled down for a good feed and soon felt much better.

'I'm sorry I was so cross,' he said, looking up at his mother, 'but it's so dull in this old hole.'

'This dull old hole is *safe*,' Mrs Aardvark said. 'Remember that. You may go up to the entrance now, but stay close to it. There's nothing like a dull old hole to dive into in time of danger.'

Pim set off up the tunnel.

When he came out at the top, he couldn't see at all at first. The sun was very bright and he sat down on his tail and blinked hard, his ears pricked up to listen for danger.

He wasn't sure what danger would sound like but the grunting sounds he heard didn't sound very dangerous. As his eyes became used to the sunlight, he saw that the grunts were coming from a band of animals which were moving around and pulling up grassheads and other plants. They were stuffing these into their mouths with their forefeet, which were much more bendy than Pim's. He tried to pull up a plant with one of his front paws, but he couldn't get hold of it at all.

Oh well, if they ate plants, they probably didn't eat aardvarks. Pim settled down to doze in the sun.

Suddenly, a voice said 'Hello!' right by his ear.

Pim sat up quickly and backed towards his burrow. He saw that one of the animals he had been watching had come up to him. He was quite small.

'Er . . . hello. What are you?' Pim asked him.

'I'm a baboon. A sort of monkey, my uncle says. What are you?'

'An aardvark.'

'An odd what?' The little baboon was staring at Pim as if he had never seen anything quite like him before.

'An *aardvark*,' said Pim clearly, 'a very

new aardvark.'

'I'm a very new baboon,' said the funny little animal, '*very* new. I don't know anything about anything yet.'

'Neither do I,' said Pim, who liked his new friend, 'except that my mother eats termites. Where do you live?'

'Where?' said the little baboon, puzzled. 'Well, everywhere. We move about all the time looking for food. At least, the grown-ups in the group do. I have milk from my mother. I like that.'

'So do I,' said Pim. 'But where do you sleep to be safe? Haven't you got a hole?'

'A hole?' said the baboon in surprise. 'No. We go up into some rocks or trees to rest.'

'Different ones every day?' said Pim. 'That must be interesting. I live in the same

old hole all the time.' He nodded towards his burrow.

'Under the ground?' The baboon peered down it doubtfully. 'Haven't you ever been up a tree?'

'A tree?' Pim asked. 'I'm not sure . . .'

'Those are trees, over there.' The little baboon pointed to them. 'There's my uncle on top of that tall one. He's look-out today.

Which reminds me – my mother will be
looking out for me.'

Just at that moment, the baboon up the
tree began to make a sharp barking noise,
and all the other baboons began to rush
about barking too.

'A lion!' squeaked Pim's new friend. 'Oh
dear, I want my mother. Oh, here she is.' A
big baboon rushed up to them. The baby

scrambled on to her back and hung on to her fur. He rode her like a jockey rides a horse as she rushed back to join the troop. They all banded together in one big family – there were other babies on their mothers' backs as well as Pim's friend – and rushed off towards the trees, barking hard.

What a fuss! All Pim had to do was go down his tunnel.

He did so. His mother opened one eye.

'What's the matter?' she said.

'Lion,' said Pim. 'The baboons warned me.'

'Ah, you've learned about baboons. They are a help. When baboons bark, you dive for home or if you're too far away you dig a hole quickly.'

'Baboons climb trees. Why don't we climb trees?'

'We can't climb. What *are* you doing? You're scratching me.'

Pim was trying to pull himself up on to his mother's back, but he kept sliding down on to her tail.

'You're the wrong shape,' he complained. 'I wanted a ride like baboons have.'

'I'm not a baboon,' said Pim's mother. 'I am a tired aardvark. Now go to sleep if you want to come with me tonight.'

Pim did want to, so he curled himself up into a little ball to sleep.

But there was something else he wanted to ask: why don't we live in a big family with lots of others, instead of just by ourselves?

He knew the answer, though.

Because he was an aardvark.

Pim went to sleep.

Big business

That night Mrs Aardvark took Pim with her on her feeding trip across the veldt. They went a different way this time. They passed through a belt of trees, or what had once been a belt of trees. Lots of them had been rooted up and thrown to the ground, and those that were still standing had their bark stripped off. There were broken branches everywhere. Pim stopped and stared around him. What could have done this? Something *huge*.

'Elephants,' said his mother. 'Oh, they *are* messy eaters. Come on. We'll go round the edge.'

'Eaters?' said Pim, following his mother. 'Do they eat aardvarks?'

'No, just grass and branches and tree bark and things. But they will throw it around so. If they fancy a branch they can't reach, they just uproot the whole tree to get at it.'

'Elephants must be very strong,' said Pim, imagining a sort of giant baboon pulling up trees with its hands. 'I don't think I want to meet an elephant.'

The termite nest which his mother chose for her dinner was near a river. Pim watched his mother tearing at the nest for a while, but an interesting smell from the river drew him like a magnet.

Soon he was bumbling along by the river bank, snuffling busily. He had to watch out for tree roots which seemed to be spread out everywhere to trip him up. A tree loomed up ahead of him, and he stepped sideways to go round it.

That was funny. Pim stopped dead. The tree had moved!

Pim shook his head briskly. Trees didn't move. He looked over his shoulder.

There were four trees moving towards him. This was too much. Pim was going back to his mother. He was about to bolt when a voice above his head said, 'Hello.'

Something nuzzled his ear. Pim looked up. Two little eyes were looking at him down

a long, long nose. Behind this
face were two great ears and a
huge body with . . . yes, the trees
were the animal's legs!

'Er . . . hello,' Pim said warily. He was still ready to run. 'What are you?'

'I'm an elephant,' said the strange creature, 'a baby elephant.'

'A *baby* elephant?' said Pim, his eyes wide. 'Your mother must be enormous.'

'Well, she is quite big,' said the baby elephant. 'I stand underneath her for shade when the sun is hot. But what are you?'

'An aardvark,' said Pim.

'An odd what?' the elephant said. He explored Pim all over with his trunk. 'You're certainly an odd something.'

'An *aardvark*,' Pim said. 'You can talk anyway. What a very odd dangly nose you've got. Stop tickling me.'

'Sorry,' said the elephant, withdrawing his trunk and holding it up. 'This is my trunk. I always use it for exploring odd . . . I mean, new things. It's very strong too. Watch.' He coiled his trunk around a small tree and yanked it right out of the ground, roots and all.

'So that's how you do it,' Pim said. 'I thought you must have hands, like baboons, for pulling things up with.' He looked at the tree on the ground. 'Aren't you going to eat it?'

'Eat it? No,' said the elephant, 'I still have milk from my mother.'

'Me too,' said Pim. He looked up at his strange new friend. 'Do elephants have holes?'

'Holes?' said the elephant. 'What would I need a hole for?'

'Well, to be safe in. Aren't you afraid of anything – lions and things?'

The baby elephant drew himself up very tall. 'The elephant is the king of the beasts.

He is afraid of nothing,' he said proudly.

Then he grinned down at Pim. 'Or so my auntie says. Actually, lions do attack baby elephants sometimes, and that's why I'm supposed to stay close to her or my mother.' He looked towards the river where there were splashing noises. 'I'd better get back to them – they're crossing the river. Would you like to come and see me off?'

Pim said he would, and that's how he came to watch a herd of elephants at bathtime.

There seemed to be elephants everywhere, squirting themselves and each other with water and churning up the mud with their huge feet. Pim's friend could hardly wait to join them. With a cheery 'Bye-ee!' he slid down the slippery mudbank and landed in the water with a great splash. A huge elephant – it must have been his mother – sploshed up to him, spanked him with her trunk and then sprayed him all over with water. Pim's friend squealed and pretended to try and run away, but he was pulled back and squirted again and again. He was obviously enjoying himself hugely.

Pim was too, as his mother saw when she found him a little later on. He was watching his friend being tugged up the steep bank on the other side of the river by his mother, while another elephant shoved him from behind. They were having quite a job getting him up the slippery slope. The king of the beasts *was* just a baby.

'So there you are,' Pim's mother said. 'Look at you. You're covered with mud. What have you been doing?'

'I got a bit splashed, that's all. Elephants

are messy bathers as well as messy eaters. Oh look, they've got him up at last.'

His friend, who was tired after his difficult scramble, had grasped his mother's tail with his trunk. She pulled him after her into the scrub.

Pim sighed. He was tired too. He turned to his mother. She had a lovely big tail, bigger than Mrs Elephant's.

'Why haven't *I* got a trunk?' he said wistfully.

'Because you're an aardvark,' said his mother. 'Come on. Home.'

A rotten digger

It was a long way home. Pim was very tired. He found it difficult to keep up with his mother, although she tried to go slowly.

At last he stopped altogether and she had to go back for him.

'Come on, Pim,' she said, 'it isn't far now.'

'My legs are squashing my feet!' he wailed. 'And my tail's heavy.'

'Oh dear,' she said, 'I forget how new you are. I know what we'll do. You needn't go any further. I'll make a new burrow right here. It seems a good place.'

While Pim blinked his tired eyes, she began to dig and dig and dig. In a few minutes the front half of her disappeared into the ground. Soon only her tail remained at the top and that was disappearing fast.

Was Pim going to be left all by himself? He was just going to tug at her tail to remind her that he was there when Mrs Aardvark backed out suddenly and nearly knocked him over.

'I hadn't forgotten you,' she said, seeing his face. 'Come on, sleepy, you'll be quite safe in here.' She began to push him into the hole she had made.

'Is this it?' said Pim. 'Is this the new burrow?' He didn't think much of it.

'No, of course it isn't. This is just a safe place where I can leave you while I'm busy digging. Now, tuck your tail in and I'll come and fetch you when our new home is ready.'

So Pim curled up snout to tail in the shallow hole and went to sleep. It was nearly light when his mother woke him up.

'Come on,' she said. 'Home.'

'I thought we weren't going home,' said Pim, stretching and coming out of his little hole.

'Not the old home, the new one,' his mother said. 'Here we are. It's right next door.'

There was an entrance tunnel and then a big roomy burrow beyond. In fact, it was exactly the same as their old home.

'Do you like it?' Pim's mother asked.

'Yes,' said Pim, 'it has a nice fresh smell.'
He settled down by his mother for his feed.
'Mm-mm. So do you.'

'Yes, I probably do smell and taste a bit
earthy,' laughed his mother. 'I'm glad you
like it.'

Pim was soon full of warm milk. He
stopped sucking, so his mouth was free to
ask questions.

'Will I be able to dig a burrow like this?'
he asked.

'Yes, dear. All aardvarks are good
diggers, if they have enough sleep, that is . . .'

Pim opened his mouth, but shut it again.
He could take a hint.

He put snout to tail and went to sleep.

★   ★   ★

He woke up feeling very lively. He couldn't
wait to practise his digging. How could he
be a proper aardvark until he could dig?
He must start now. And there was a good
place to begin – the shelter his mother had
made the night before. There was one snag
though. His mother was still fast asleep, so
he couldn't ask her permission. Well, his plan
was a safe one. He was sure she wouldn't
mind. He crept past her and into the tunnel.

He was surprised to find that it was still
light outside. In fact, it was only late afternoon,
but that made no difference to his plan.

He sat on his tail and put up his ears and
listened carefully. It seemed to be safe. He
scampered over to the shallow burrow and went
inside. Yes, the earth was still nice and soft. He
stretched out his forefeet with their powerful

claws and began to dig. Oh, this was easy.

But after a little while he began to realise that it was not as easy as all that. He soon found that he had a pile of earth under his tummy which got in the way. What did he do with it? The further forward he burrowed, the more earth he had piled up round him, under him and behind him. It had to go somewhere.

Then he remembered the shower of earth he'd had to dodge when he was watching his mother digging. She had kicked it out behind her with her hind legs. Pim began to kick.

But he had left it too late. His mother kicked it out behind her as she went along, so she never had more than a manageable amount to deal with at a time. Pim already had a small mountain behind him. He kicked harder and harder, but only succeeded in burying himself in it.

Poor Pim. He lay still, panting. Now what was he going to do? He had blocked the way out behind him. He would have to turn round and burrow his way out.

When he felt strong enough he would begin. . . . But what was that? There was something moving outside, just above him, something with a strong smell. He had never smelt it before but he knew what it was. Big cat smell – leopard or lion. It was the smell of danger.

Pim froze. He was only just under the ground. If the big cat heard him, it could probably reach him. Pim didn't want to end up as a tasty tea for a lion.

But now he was really stuck. He dare not burrow any deeper into the ground because

he was such a rotten digger and anyway
he might be heard. He couldn't go back to
the surface and make a dive for his safe den
with the big cat wandering about up there.

He was trapped. He would have to stay
here until it was safe to come out.

Suddenly his ears pricked up and quivered.
There were scraping sounds in the earth in
front of him! Was the lion coming down for
him that way? Pim was so frightened that he
couldn't think any more. He just crouched
there shivering with his eyes shut, while the
sounds got nearer and nearer.

Something burst through the wall of
earth in front of him. It was upon him!

'Pim?' his mother's voice whispered.

'I guessed you were here. Come on. I've made a tunnel.'

In a few moments Pim was safe in his burrow, cuddled close to his mother.

He told her all about what had happened and how he had thought she was a lion coming for him.

'Lions are rotten diggers,' his mother said. 'Anyway, what's this for?' She tweaked his trembling snout. 'If you had used this, you would have known it was me and not the lion. Well, never mind. It's all over now. Come and have your feed.'

Pim snuggled close to her and found a teat to suck. But before he took it in his mouth, he said, 'Are you sure I'm an aardvark?'

'Yes,' said his mother, 'quite sure.'

'Well, you said all aardvarks are good

diggers. You were wrong. I'm a terrible digger.'

Mrs Aardvark smiled. 'Well, I should have said "except when they're very young". You haven't been taught to dig yet. I'll give you a lesson tomorrow.'

'And then I'll be a proper aardvark?'

'Pim, you *are* an aardvark. Nothing can change that.'

But Pim wasn't absolutely sure.

A long story

Pim was tired after his adventure, so his mother left him to sleep it off while she went out to find some termites. He was just waking up when she got back.

'Yes, I went without you,' she said, before he could start complaining, 'and it's a good job I did too. This is a dangerous place. We'll have to go back to our old burrow. We're very near a water-hole here.'

'Water's not dangerous,' said Pim. 'The elephants had a lot of fun in it.'

'Water is dangerous to us when it attracts so many animals. They come to drink there every evening, hundreds of them. It's the only drinking place for miles. That means there are lions going right past our front door.'

'Like yesterday!' said Pim. 'Like the one that frightened me yesterday.'

'That's right,' said his mother. 'We shall have to move again, which is a pity because there are lots of good termite nests in this area. Oh well, I must get some sleep.'

'I've *been* asleep,' Pim complained. 'I feel awake now. I couldn't sleep any more.'

'Well, you can go up to the top and sun yourself for a bit if you like, as you did the other morning, but stay very close to the burrow.

In fact, keep your tail in the entrance tunnel.'

Pim bounded towards the tunnel and then stopped and came back. He had remembered something.

'Perhaps I won't go up after all. There might be lions.'

'Not at this time of the morning. They're lazy beasts.' Mrs Aardvark smiled. 'Not everything wants to eat you, you know. You'll be all right if you do what you're told.'

Pim crept slowly up the tunnel. He peeped out and blinked. The sun had just risen and was already very bright. He pricked up his ears and listened carefully. Nothing. With most of him still inside the tunnel, Pim sat himself down. The sun was lovely and warm.

Sunbathing made him drowsy, and certainly his ears were not as pricked as they should have been or he might have heard his visitor coming. But it didn't bound, or hop or gallop. In fact it had no legs at all, so it just wriggled towards him through the grass very slowly.

The first thing Pim knew about it was when something tickled his ear. He put up a back foot and scratched the tickly place. He felt something there.

'You don't have to kick me,' said a voice.

'Sorry. I thought you were an itch,' Pim said. He looked at his visitor. He seemed harmless enough – long and bendy like an elephant's trunk without the elephant. He had better make sure though.

'Do you want to eat me?' he asked, backing slowly into the burrow.

'Not particularly,' said the long, thin

creature. 'You look a bit too big for me, and anyway I'm not hungry at the moment. Pythons don't eat very often.'

'Pythons? Is that what you are?' Pim stopped backing and took a good look at his visitor.

'Yes, I'm a python. What are you?'

'An aardvark.'

'An odd what?'

Pim was getting rather tired of people making this rude remark. 'An *aardvark*!'

'Oh, you look a bit piggy to me. Wait a minute. Aard-vark – earth-pig. That's what it means. You *are* a sort of pig.'

'Do pigs eat termites?' asked
Pim. He wasn't a bit insulted about
being called a pig – just interested.
'Aardvarks eat termites. At least
grown-up ones do. My mother
eats them every night.'

'Oh?' The python had no idea what
termites were, but he wasn't going to admit
it. 'Your mother . . . do you see her often

then? I only saw mine once. Just after I'd hatched. She . . . Whoops! I think it's gone!'

'What's gone?' Pim stared at the little snake, who was searching the grass in front of him.

'My wiggly tooth. My egg tooth. Didn't you have one when you hatched? A special tooth for slitting the shell of your egg so that you could get out.'

'Er . . . I expect I did,' said Pim. 'I don't remember. Did you say you've only seen your mother once? Who feeds you then? Who looks after you?'

'I look after myself,' said the python. 'I don't expect I'll need feeding for months, and then I shall wrap myself round something and squash it and swallow it whole.' The little python couldn't resist teasing Pim a little. 'Something like you, I should think. You'd be very tasty.'

Pim backed hurriedly into the burrow. The python was only a little chap but . . .

With a wicked glint in his eye, the python followed him a little way.

'May I practise on you?' he asked. 'It would be awfully helpful of you and I'd try not to squash you too much.'

Pim didn't feel like being awfully helpful. He turned and bolted down his hole. Mrs Aardvark opened one eye as her son scuttled in.

'Well, who wanted to eat you?' she asked.

'A python,' said Pim. His mother sat bolt upright. 'Oh, it was only a little one, but he said he thought I'd be tasty.'

'I daresay,' said Mrs Aardvark. 'You keep away from pythons. Big ones anyway.'

'This one had only just hatched,' said Pim.

'His egg tooth fell out while we were talking.'

'Oh, he was just a baby then.' Mrs Aardvark settled back in her sleeping position. Pim curled up too, but there was one more thing he wanted to ask.

'Was I hatched? I don't remember.'

'No. You were born.'

'What's born?'

'Well, you grew in my tummy and when you were ready to arrive, I landed you just as you are, not in an egg.'

Pim snuggled close to his mother. He thought about the poor little python who had to crack his way out of an egg by himself and had nobody to look after him or feed him or belong to.

'I'm glad I'm an aardvark,' Pim said. 'I'm glad I was born.'

An ugly business

Late that evening, Pim and his mother crept out of their burrow and stood listening, ears and noses a-quiver. There had been a lot of traffic past their door earlier on – every animal in Africa seemed to be going to the water-hole – but now it was safe to come out.

'Come on,' Mrs Aardvark whispered. 'Keep close to me.'

Pim had every intention of keeping close

to his mother. There were lots of strange smells about and he could hear odd bellows and roars in the distance. This was no place to linger by himself.

They galloped across the veldt towards their old burrow. It wasn't really very far. Pim began to get excited when he recognised his old home ground.

'There's the baboons' look-out tree!' he shouted. 'We're there.'

He ran on ahead. 'I'll be first home,' he called over his shoulder.

But he had a shock when he bounded up to the burrow. Someone was there before him. An animal with an incredibly ugly face was blocking the entrance. It was standing there with great curving tusks pointing towards Pim! It looked very fierce indeed.

Pim backed away and ran to his mother.
'Mum! Keep away! There's a thing, a
horrible thing . . .'

'With tusks?' his mother asked. 'And an ugly face? Oh, it's just a warthog. I should have known that this might happen. The lazy things will always take over one of our burrows rather than dig a home for themselves. I expect it's a lady warthog who wants to have her babies there. We'll have to dig a new one, that's all.'

'You mean you're going to let her have it?' Pim said. 'Our burrow?'

'Do you feel like arguing with those tusks?' Mrs Aardvark said. 'I don't. Anyway you should be proud. It's because we are the best diggers in Africa that other animals want our dens.'

Pim thought about that as they moved on looking for a good place to make a burrow.

'Here we are,' his mother said at last. 'I

like this place.' She looked around at the sandy soil in the sheltered spot she had chosen. They were on a slight hill and would have a good view of the surrounding country.

'Mum,' Pim said. 'If we didn't dig such good burrows, other animals wouldn't want them, would they? We could keep them for ourselves. That would be much nicer.'

'Don't be silly, dear,' his mother said. 'Come on. I'll give you a digging lesson.'

'I'm not sure that I want to be a good digger,' Pim said stubbornly, sitting on his tail. 'If I make rotten burrows when I'm grown up, nobody will steal them, will they?'

'No, perhaps not. But the roof will probably fall in on you and you'll be buried alive. Or when you're caught far from your rotten burrow by an enemy, you won't be able to dig fast enough to get away from it. Either way, you won't last long. Please yourself. You needn't learn to dig if you don't want to.'

She turned away.

Pim decided that he did want to.

'All right,' he said. 'You can teach me to dig if you like. It might come in useful.'

So Pim had his digging lesson. He was taught how to sweep away with his back feet and his tail the earth he had dug up with his forefeet. He was also taught to fold down his ears. This was to keep the earth out of them.

'I wish I had known about this yesterday,' he said. 'It's very tickly, earth in the ears.'

'Yes,' his mother said. 'But you can pop them back up again now. It's time I made the burrow. Now watch.'

She began to dig at enormous speed.

Earth and stones flew into the air behind her in a great shower.

She stopped and came up to see if Pim was all right.

He had his ears folded down and his eyes tight shut.

'What have you got your eyes shut for?' she said. 'How can you watch like that?'

'Because earth in the eyes is uncomfortable too,' he said. 'Have *you* ever tried to watch another aardvark digging? I'm all battered.'

'I'm sorry, dear,' Mrs Aardvark said. 'But you don't have to stand right in the line of fire, you know. Move over there a bit. That's right. I shan't be long.'

She dived in again and there was a new burrow waiting in no time at all. Mrs Aardvark came up to invite Pim to come and inspect it.

'Well?' she said. 'Will it do?'

'It will do,' said Pim, looking round at the neat chamber under the ground. 'If I were a warthog, I just couldn't wait to come and pinch it.'

'Pim!' Mrs Aardvark said warningly. 'Go and build yourself a rotten den then. Go on, cleversticks!'

'I will,' Pim said. 'When I can dig as well as you I will, but this will do for now.' He grinned at his mother. 'When I'm grown up I'll build a burrow that every animal in Africa will want for his own, not just a few ugly old warthogs. All the animals will know that I'm the best digger in the world. Can I have my feed now?'

'Yes,' his mother said, settling down on the earth floor. 'You may. So you've decided to be a good digger after all, have you?'

'Yes,' said Pim with his mouth full. Then he leaned back and looked up at his mother. 'Well, I can't help it, can I? I'm an aardvark.'

A tall story

Mrs Aardvark spent the rest of the night hunting for termite hills. Pim didn't go with her as he was tired after his digging lesson. He went to sleep in the new burrow and, of course, he was just waking up as his mother came home at dawn to sleep.

'All right,' she said when she saw his hopeful face, 'after your feed you can go up top for a while. Don't be too long though: I'm ready for a good day's sleep.'

Soon Pim was scampering up the tunnel. He popped his head out and listened. Nothing.

He ventured out a little further when his night eyes had become used to the light. This was an interesting place. The new burrow was on a sort of shelf. There were what looked like the tops of trees scalloping the edge of it, and beyond them the veldt stretched out as far as he could see.

Suddenly he heard something. There was a sort of munching noise coming from the treetops. Monkeys?

Very cautiously, his tail leaving a trail in the sand, Pim moved towards the sound. As he neared the edge of the shelf, which was really a small cliff, Pim saw that the sound was being made by a long, pink tongue plucking leaves from a tree.

The owner of the tongue saw Pim at the same time as Pim saw her. Shyly she jerked back her head which was balanced on a long, long neck that seemed to go down for ever. Pim couldn't help staring. He peeped over the edge of the cliff. She went right down to the ground below! She had not climbed up the tree as he had at first thought. She was as tall as the tree!

Pim forgot about being polite.

'What *are* you?' he said, goggling.

'Me? I'm just a giraffe.' She smiled at Pim in a friendly way. 'Haven't you seen a giraffe before?'

'No, I haven't,' Pim said. 'You . . . you're very tall, aren't you?'

'I suppose I am. I have to be to reach my food. I've never seen anyone like you either.

What are you?'

'An aardvark.' Pim waited for the usual reply.

'An odd . . .? I'm sorry, I didn't quite catch it.'

Well, this was a change at any rate. Mind you, Miss Giraffe was in no position to find anyone else an oddity.

'An *aardvark*,' Pim said clearly. 'I live under the ground, and you live a long way above it.'

'Well yes,' Miss Giraffe admitted. 'I find reaching down to the ground rather difficult, actually. Drinking is terribly difficult. My legs are so long and my knees won't bend properly. I have to straddle them out sideways and bend my head down in between them to the water. It's a good job I have a long neck.'

'Show me,' Pim said.
Miss Giraffe showed
him, which was very kind of
her, seeing that it was such an
uncomfortable position for her.
'Yes, I see what you mean,'
Pim said when her head came up
again. 'How do you get down to
sleep? It must be very difficult.'
'I don't,' Miss Giraffe said.
'I sleep standing up.'

'Oh,' Pim said. 'Do you know, I probably would never have met you at all if I hadn't been up here on this cliff. Not to talk to.'

'Now, you show me something,' Miss Giraffe said.

That foxed him. 'What sort of something?' he asked.

'Well, something special that you can do because you're an aardvark.'

Pim thought hard. 'Well, I can dig,' he said. 'Can you dig?'

'No,' said Miss Giraffe. 'Show me.'

So Pim, delighted to show off, dug a hole very fast, shooting earth into the air behind him with his hind legs and tail.

Miss Giraffe was very impressed.

'But why are your ears all flat like that?' she said when he popped his head out of the hole again. 'You do look funny.'

'Keeps the earth out,' Pim said. He had thought of something else he could do. 'I can stick my tongue in and out very fast,' he said. 'Watch!'

'I can do that too,' Miss Giraffe said. 'There. My tongue is just as long as yours.'

And so began a tongue-sticking-out match. That is how poor sleepy Mrs Aardvark found them when she came out to see why Pim had been such a long time.

'Really, Pim,' she said. 'You are very

rude! I apologise for my son's manners, Miss Giraffe. He should know better.'

'Oh, that's all right, Mrs Aardvark,' Miss Giraffe said, winking at Pim. 'I asked him to. But I must go now. My mother will be looking for me. Goodbye.' She turned and galloped away, her head and neck swaying forwards and backwards in a steady rhythm.

Pim watched her go quite sadly.

'She was nice,' he told his mother, 'but I'm glad I don't have to sleep standing up.'

'I shall be grateful to get any sleep at all today,' Mrs Aardvark snapped, 'even if I have to stand on my head.'

Pim decided that it would be unwise to keep her from the burrow any longer.

A fast one

Mrs Aardvark got her sleep. She and Pim slept all day and then they were ready at nightfall for their termite hunt.

They came out of the tunnel into bright moonlight. It was almost as light as day.

'We'll have to be very careful tonight,' Mrs Aardvark said as they moved off. 'There'll be a lot of predators about.'

'Predators?' said Pim. 'What are they?'

'Well, they're animals that may fancy an aardvark for supper,' Mrs Aardvark said. 'Lions and leopards and cheetahs . . .'

'I haven't heard of them. What's a cheetah?'

'Oh, another sort of big cat. They're very fast runners. Faster than anything I have ever seen.'

Pim looked down at his clumsy feet lolloping along. 'How do we get away from them then?'

'The usual way. Find a hole to shelter in or dig one quickly. If we're really cornered, we can always fight, of course. I had to fight a cheetah once.'

'Did you win?' asked Pim, gazing at his mother wide-eyed.

'I did,' she said grimly. 'I wouldn't be here otherwise. But I was lucky. It's best to get away from them by digging if you can.'

Pim looked about him fearfully. He did not fancy his chances of digging faster than a cheetah could run, even if he saw one coming a long way away.

'I think you'd better teach me how to fight. Soon!' he said.

'All right,' his mother said. 'I suppose it's about time you learned, although if you didn't keep wandering off by yourself it wouldn't be necessary. I'm here to defend you – that's what mothers are for.'

'Oh good,' Pim said, moving very close to her. 'If a cheetah chases us, will you dig us a hole or fight it?' He was rather looking forward to watching a good fight.

'Wait and see,' said his mother. 'It may never happen.'

It didn't. They reached a patch of termite hills without even smelling 'big cat', never mind hearing any distant roars. Pim was almost disappointed.

'Now, don't go wandering off,' said his mother as she set about breaching a tall termite nest. 'You stay near me.'

Pim looked around him. There were some very interesting looking bushes by a funny shaped tree just across the clearing.

'Can I go over there?' he asked. 'I'll be very good and not go any further.'

His mother broke off her attack on the nest and looked at the bushes.

'All right,' she said. 'But come back at once if you hear or smell anything dangerous.'

Pim scampered over to the bushes. There was nothing there.

Not at first, that is. He had only been there a few minutes when a tangled ball of young animals came rolling past him – he was hidden from them by a bush – making squeaking noises. They were obviously fighting each other, or rather playing at fighting each other.

One of them broke away from the others and climbed on to a low branch of the tree. Pim could see him more clearly. It looked as if he had been crying black tears – he had two dark lines from his eyes down to his mouth. He was covered with spots. The fur on his back was long and fluffy but underneath he was smooth and dark. He was balancing on the branch with the help of a long, spotted tail.

Suddenly he sprang down, tumbling his brothers and sisters in all directions. They turned on him with little growls and squeaks.

The fighting got quite fierce.

Pim was dying to join in; they were having such fun.

There was just one thing bothering him, though. They were quite small and didn't look a bit dangerous, but they smelled . . . well, catty. He was an aardvark after all and 'cat' meant danger.

But now they didn't look a bit dangerous. They had stopped scuffling and were all cuddled together. One of them was licking the smallest one; perhaps he had come off worst in the fight. The others were making a nice soft purring sound. A very peaceful and contented sound it seemed to Pim. Surely they couldn't be cats!

He had to find out. Pim came out from behind his bush and walked towards them.

When they saw him they jumped up and huddled together. The biggest one said, 'What are you?'

'An aardvark,' Pim said. 'I was just wondering . . .'

'An odd what?' the spotted animal said, and the others tittered.

'An *aardvark*,' Pim said. 'I eat termites.'

'Oh, we're cheetahs,' the cub said, 'and we eat aardvarks!'

'Not this one, you don't,' said Pim, turning and bolting back to his mother.

The cheetah cubs pretended to chase him but they were tired after their fight and, of course, they were much too young to eat aardvarks.

When she saw Pim running towards her, Mrs Aardvark quickly swallowed her last termite.

'Cheetahs!' gasped Pim.

'In here then!' said his mother, and shoved him inside the empty termite nest. With great speed she dug herself deep into the ground.

Just in time. The cubs' mother came back and smelled aardvark. But she soon lost interest when she couldn't find them and, anyway, she had a hungry family to feed.

When she had gone, Mrs Aardvark collected Pim and they galloped home across the veldt.

'How did you know that cheetah was coming?' Mrs Aardvark asked Pim.

'Er . . . because I'm an aardvark,' he said loftily. 'I smelled it.'

His mother was not impressed.

'Rubbish,' she said, 'that's a whopper. Now tell me the truth.'

So Pim told her all about it.

A spiky one

Next evening Mrs Aardvark gave Pim a fighting lesson outside the burrow.

'Mind you, I don't think I really need to tell you what to do,' Pim's mother said as they went up the tunnel. 'Instinct will tell you.'

'Who's instinct?' Pim said.

'*What's* instinct,' Mrs Aardvark said. 'Well, it's the voice inside you that tells you important things you need to know.

Remember when the lion came sniffing about when you were trapped under the ground? You couldn't see it, but I expect you could smell it. Well, how did you know that it was a big cat?'

'I just knew,' Pim said.

'Yes. Well, that was instinct working. Now, let's see if it will work for you again. I'm going to be a cheetah.'

'A lion,' Pim said.

'All right, I'm a lion. Now you stand over there under that tree. I'll pounce on you suddenly. I think you'll know what to do.'

'Will you roar?' Pim thought this was a good game.

'No, I can't. You'll have to imagine that bit. Now, I'm a lion, remember.'

Pim stood in front of the tree and waited. His mother *was* a long time. He looked up.

This was a funny tree with a long thin trunk and the top spreading out like an umbrella. There was something moving up there. Was it a bird or a squirrel? Pim peered a bit harder.

Mrs Aardvark pounced.

At once Pim rolled over on to his back and began lashing at her with all four feet, his claws fully out. He even struck at her with his tail.

'All right!' Mrs Aardvark gasped, trying to hold him off. 'I'm just your mother. Stop.'

Pim sat up slowly.

'You said you were a lion,' he grumbled. 'I wish you'd make up your mind.'

His mother looked at him.

'I'm glad I'm not a lion,' she said, 'if that's how you treat them.'

Pim suddenly realized. 'I *knew*!' he shouted. 'I knew how to fight!'

'You knew all right,' said his mother, feeling the tender spots all over her. 'It's a good job I have a very thick hide. If I'd had a thin skin like a cat I would have been scratched and ripped and torn. Ugh!'

Pim was very pleased with himself.

'Isn't instinct wonderful?' he cried. 'Shall we have another fight tomorrow?'

'No, thank you,' Mrs Aardvark said. 'That's your last fighting lesson.'

'But it's only my first fighting lesson,' said Pim.

'It's the first and the last,' his mother said firmly. She felt very sore. 'Come on. If we're to find some termite nests before dawn, we must get going.'

And so that night and the next one and every night for the next five months, Pim accompanied his mother on her hunting trips. He also grew bigger and stronger.

He practised digging a lot and became quite expert. They moved house several times and each time Pim helped his mother dig the new burrow.

But one night Mrs Aardvark said, 'I don't want you to help me this time.'

'Why not?' said Pim. 'I know what to do.'

'Yes, you do. So you can make yourself a burrow, can't you?'

Pim beamed at her. 'Yes! Yes, I will.'

So Pim dug his first burrow. He made a long tunnel and then dug out a round chamber at the end of it big enough to turn round in.

Proudly he brought his mother down to inspect it.

'Yes, it's good,' she said, looking round her.

'I thought you said you were going to build rotten burrows that warthogs wouldn't want.'

'If any warthog tries to pinch this, he will have me to reckon with,' Pim said fiercely.

It wasn't a warthog, it was a porcupine. Pim met him coming down the tunnel the next evening. The porcupine backed hastily in front of Pim.

'I'm s-sorry. I didn't know anybody lived here,' he said. 'I-I didn't mean to intrude. Really I didn't.' His quills rattled nervously.

'What made you think you could just walk in here when you felt like it?' Pim said fiercely. 'You've got a cheek!'

'Oh d-dear,' said the little porcupine. 'My mother t-t-told me that empty aardvark b-burrows make the b-b-best homes, you see.'

'This aardvark burrow isn't empty,'
Pim said.

'No, I-I can see that,' said the little
porcupine, his quills rattling more than ever.
'I-I'll g-go at once.' He turned and began to
rattle away with a sharp shuffling gait.

'Wait!' Pim said. 'I forgive you. Please
come back, little . . . what are you?'

'A porcupine.' The creature came back slowly.

'What can you do?' Pim asked. 'I'm just interested.'

'D-do?' the porcupine said. 'Well, I can climb trees and swim.'

'Swim?'

'Yes, you know, m-move in the water to cross rivers and p-pools. Can you swim?'

'Er . . . of course,' said Pim. 'What else can you do? Can you fight?'

'Of course,' said the little porcupine. 'I make my quills stand up like this, and then I rush at my attacker – like this.' He charged at Pim, but stopped just short of him.

Pim was very relieved. It would have been very painful indeed to have all those sharp quills stuck into him at once.

'Yes, I see,' he said. 'Er . . . what do you eat?'

'Oh, grass and bark and things like that. What do you eat?'

'Termites,' Pim said. 'I was just going to hunt for some as a matter of fact.'

'Oh, well I won't keep you then. Goodbye. Thank you for being so nice.' The porcupine shuffled off.

He happened to look round a second or two later, in time to see the friendly aardvark turning into another burrow. That was a funny place to look for termites. Oh well, it was nothing to do with him. The porcupine continued on his way.

He wasn't to know that Pim wasn't weaned yet; that he was heading for his mother and some milk.

The last one

Pim went out with his mother after his feed
as usual.

Mrs Aardvark had a problem. Pim was
six months old now, which is quite grown up
for an aardvark, and it was time he began
to eat termites.

But Pim wasn't interested in termites. She
had taught him to tear open their nests. She
had taught him to close his nostrils to keep

the insects out while he was working. She had taught him how to use his tongue. But she couldn't teach him to want to eat termites, and while he was full of milk, hunger wouldn't drive him to try them.

There was only one thing to do, and when they got back to her burrow Mrs Aardvark did it.

'Good night, Pim,' she said, as she stopped at the entrance to her burrow.

'Good night already?' Pim said. 'What about my feed?'

'Oh, you're too grown up for milk now. I'm not going to feed you any more. Good night, dear.'

She turned her back and disappeared down her entrance tunnel. She felt terribly mean but it was the only way.

Pim went down his entrance tunnel feeling very cross indeed. How could his mother refuse to feed him just like that? What a cruel thing to do. He felt very hard-done-by and muttered to himself as he dropped off to sleep.

His mother hardly slept at all. She lay there worrying about him all day.

When Pim woke up that evening he was hungry, but he couldn't bring himself to go to his mother's burrow and be refused again. He lay there sulking and wondering what to do.

Suddenly he heard something, something he had never heard before. It sounded like thousands of tiny feet marching! It couldn't be. He listened very carefully. There was no doubt about it – tiny footfalls – that's what he could hear. Pim dashed up the tunnel to see what it could be. His ears must be playing tricks.

They weren't. Not far from the burrow there was a long wavy line of termites marching. Pim knew what they were by the smell, even before he was near enough to see what they were. Termites on the march, thousands of them!

And for the first time Pim saw them as they really were – *food*! Food marching right past his front door! He wouldn't even have to go searching for it. Food that he didn't have to dig for.

It was just too easy. All he had to do was put out his long sticky tongue . . .

M-m-m-m! They were really very good. He shot out his tongue again and again. Soon he was gobbling termites as fast as he could go.

Mrs Aardvark had also heard the termites and come up, but when she saw Pim she stayed where she was. At last! She needn't worry about him any more. He liked termites.

Pim *did* like termites, and there wasn't much left of that wavy line of them by the time he had eaten his fill.

As he went back towards his burrow he saw his mother watching him.

'It's all right,' he said. 'I'm a grown-up aardvark now. I shan't need you any more.' Suddenly he galloped over to her. 'If you hurry up you can still catch some termites. I didn't eat them all.'

'Oh good,' said Mrs Aardvark. 'Thank you, my son.' She galloped happily away to chase the tail of the termite column. Her job was done.

Pim crawled into his burrow. He settled down in his sleeping corner, tired and happy and full. Oh, termites *were* delicious. Tomorrow night he would go out hunting and find some more – lots more.

Pim looked around him at the firm earth walls of his home. Yes, this was a good burrow – and he had made it all himself.

He sighed happily and buried his snout in his tail.

There was no doubt about it now.

Pim was an aardvark.

This is Suzy.

Suzy is a small stripy cat.

Suzy likes: living in France, chasing butterflies and being stroked the wrong way.

Suzy doesn t like: getting lost . . .

Read another Jill Tomlinson and find out more.

This is Plop.

Plop is a baby barn owl.

He is fat and fluffy.

He has big, round eyes.

He has soft, downy feathers.

He is perfect in every way,

except for just ONE thing . . .

Read another Jill Tomlinson
and find out more.

This is Hilda.

Hilda is a small, speckled hen.

Hilda likes cornflakes, fire-engines and visiting her auntie.

But there is one thing that Hilda would like more than anything else . . .

Read another Jill Tomlinson and find out more.

This is Pat.

Pat is a little sea otter.

She loves asking questions.

But what happens when
no one knows the answers?

Clever Pat just has to find
things out for herself!

Read another Jill Tomlinson
and find out more.

EGMONT PRESS: ETHICAL PUBLISHING

Egmont Press is about turning writers into successful authors and children into passionate readers – producing books that enrich and entertain. As a responsible children's publisher, we go even further, considering the world in which our consumers are growing up.

Safety First
Naturally, all of our books meet legal safety requirements. But we go further than this; every book with play value is tested to the highest standards – if it fails, it's back to the drawing-board.

Made Fairly
We are working to ensure that the workers involved in our supply chain – the people that make our books – are treated with fairness and respect.

Responsible Forestry
We are committed to ensuring all our papers come from environmentally and socially responsible forest sources.

For more information, please visit our website at
www.egmont.co.uk/ethicalpublishing

The Forest Stewardship Council (FSC) is an international, non-governmental organisation dedicated to promoting responsible management of the world's forests. FSC operates a system of forest certification and product labelling that allows consumers to identify wood and wood-based products from well-managed forests.

For more information about the FSC, please visit their website at www.fsc-uk.org

FSC
Mixed Sources
Product group from well-managed forests and other controlled sources
Cert no. TT-COC-002332
www.fsc.org
© 1996 Forest Stewardship Council